Bumper Book of Laughs

Gyles Brandreth

Illustrated by Colin Hawkins,
Robert Nixon, Sara Silcock

MADCAP

Also available:

Bumper Book of Brainteasers
Bumper Book of Horror
Bumper Book of Magic

Published in Great Britain in 1999 by
Madcap Books, André Deutsch Ltd,
76 Dean Street, London, W1V 5HA
www.vci.co.uk

Text copyright © 1999 Madcap Books/Gyles Brandreth
Illustrations copyright © Colin Hawkins, Robert Nixon
and Sara Silcock

A catalogue record for this title is available
from the British Library

ISBN 0 233 99569 2

Typesetting by Falcon Oast Graphic Art
Printed and bound in Great Britain by
Mackays of Chatham plc

Contents

INTRODUCTION

Making people laugh is a wonderful gift. Some people have it naturally - and are funny without having to think about it. But most of us aren't that lucky. We'd like to be funny because it is such fun being funny, but we aren't quite sure of the best way to set about it. That's why I've written this book. It is packed with practical ideas, games to play, jokes to tell, silly poems to recite, all of which should help you to make your family and friends smile, chuckle and even occasionally roar out loud!

You can be funny in so many different ways. Telling funny stories is probably the most popular, and jokes come in all sorts of shapes and sizes. You can learn the Quick Quip:

A bee's just a humbug!

or the Short Story:

There were two men riding on a train for the first time ever. They had some bananas they'd brought with them to eat on board. Just when they were peeling the bananas the train went into a very dark tunnel.

The first man shouted out in the darkness, 'Have you eaten your banana yet?'

'No,' the friend replied.

'Well, don't touch it!' warned the first man. 'I took one bite and went blind!'

Then there is the Long Joke, which is too long to put here, so I won't mention it! You need to memorise Long Jokes carefully and make sure you deliver the punchlines clearly and with just the right emphasis. Never rush through the story and never tell the same Long Joke to the same audience twice.

Practise your jokes as much as you can - it's only by trying out different ones that you'll learn which kind you tell best. You might find that people laugh at you more when you tell Long Jokes rather than Quick Quips, or when you do funny things; you'll just have to experiment.

Sometimes people laugh at you when you're *not* trying to be funny. Although it may be annoying for you to drop a heavy book on your toe, everyone watching could find it hilarious - even your friends. After the first yelp of pain try to laugh with them, and keep them laughing with a joke - the one about the man who dropped a detective story on his toe, shouted in pain and said angrily, 'I thought it was supposed to be *light* reading!'

With a bit of luck people will also laugh at you when you try to do funny things. These can be very simple, like wearing a false nose or mask, or something that takes worthwhile time - putting on a play, organising a treasure hunt, or dressing up.

I was brought up on the saying 'There's a time and place for everything,' but there are very few occasions when humour does not help. If a friend is ill, you can try cheering him up with your collection of printing errors (see page 37). If your younger brother or sister is bored, amuse them with a ridiculous riddle. If your mother is annoyed at you for spilling orange squash all over her best sofa, you could try to make her smile with a joke:

'Doctor, doctor, I feel like a dog.'
'Well, sit down and tell me about it.'
'I can't, doctor. I'm not allowed on the furniture.'

However, this might make matters worse - so be careful!

Serious things can be faced more easily if you can find the humour in them. Going to the dentist can be a very serious business, but try to remember the funny side:

'I said DON'T SWALLOW' yelled the dentist. 'That was my *last* pair of pliers.'

That couldn't have really happened (could it?), but some very odd things *do* happen in real life, and sometimes even make the papers! There was the report, for instance, of a man who went to bed, stubbed his cigarette out on his plastic false teeth, and started a blaze so huge that the fire brigade had to come and put it out. All you have to do to be funny is to keep a watchful eye on the news, and remember things like that.

People also *say* very strange things. I was visiting a school recently and heard someone explain, 'I always find my feet are too big for other people's stairs ...' If you hear it, write it down! Keep a notebook handy and everywhere you go be ready to jot down things that strike you as funny: odd road signs; the funny things you hear on buses; silly advertisements on hoardings or on the television; funny things that happen to you. The more you look, the more you'll see - watch the way people talk, walk, behave. Listen to what they say and how they say it.

Whatever you do, DO NOT make jokes at someone else's expense. Don't try to be funny if your best friend's dog has just been run over. WAIT UNTIL THE TIME IS RIGHT before you launch into your jokes, impersonations and charades. And DO watch people carefully to see what makes them laugh. When others are chuckling at the television or in the cinema you should keep one eye on them and remember the sort of thing that amuses them most. After all, their idea of what's funny may be different from yours. To be really funny, you have to be able to make *everyone* laugh, so the more you watch, listen, write down and memorise, the better at it you'll be.

Have fun!

BAD JOKES

'Bad' means that these jokes will make you groan rather than laugh - it doesn't mean that they're no good! Lots of people love Bad Jokes because they know just what to expect.

What is all this groaning really about? A lot of it is caused by odd words called 'puns'. To explain a pun, it's best to demonstrate how one works. You ask, 'Why do leopards never escape from the zoo?' The answer is, of course, 'Because they're always spotted.' 'Spotted' means both that they have spots and that they are seen. This is a pun, and for you to make your own Bad Jokes, you need to know how to make puns, too. Some useful words to start with are:

saw	change
ruler	dough (doe)
horse (hoarse)	light
well	spring
roll	great (grate)

As you see, the words don't have to be spelt the same as long as they sound the same. Sometimes you can have words that are quite different:

Did you hear about the cat who swallowed a ball of wool?
She had mittens!

So, as well as learning these jokes by heart, make up your own; and when your chance comes you can start telling them in a long breathless string, not waiting for anyone to laugh before you go on to the next! That way, you'll never know whether they would have laughed, groaned or stayed silent!

What do you do if someone offers you rock cakes?
Take your pick.

What animal is it best to be on a cold day?
A little otter.

What language do twins speak in Holland?
Double Dutch.

What does the sea say to the sand?
Nothing, it just waves.

If you dug a hole in the middle of the road what would come up?
A policeman.

Why are oysters lazy?
Because they are always found in beds.

How many peas are there in a pint?
One.

What would happen if you swallowed a frog?
You might croak.

What kind of puzzle makes people angry?
A crossword puzzle.

Did you hear about the fight on the bus?
The conductor punched a ticket.

Why is an operation funny?
Because it leaves the patient in stitches.

What do you say to a man who is two metres tall and in a nasty temper?
Sir.

What kind of bulbs should you never water?
Light bulbs.

Why does the Statue of Liberty stand in New York Harbour?
Because she can't sit down.

How was spaghetti invented?
Someone used his noodle.

What would you do if you swallowed a pen?
Use a pencil.

What's the first thing you put into a pie?
Your teeth.

What happened at the flea circus?
A dog came and stole the show.

Is it true that a lion won't attack you if you're carrying an umbrella?
That depends on how fast you're carrying it.

What is a three-season bed?
One without a spring.

What tree does everyone carry around with him?
A palm.

What did the dirt say when it rained?
If this keeps up, my name's mud.

How is a doormat related to a doorstep?
It's a stepfather.

How can a leopard change its spots?
By moving.

Why did the boy sleep on the chandelier?
Because he was a light sleeper.

Why did the store hire a cross-eyed man as detective?
Because the customers wouldn't know which way he was looking.

FOREMAN: 'Why are you only carrying one plank when the other men are carrying two?'
WORKER: 'Well, they're too lazy to make a double journey like I do.'

JUDGE: 'You claim you robbed the grocery store because you were starving. So why didn't you take the food instead of the cash out of the till?'
ACCUSED: 'I'm a proud man, Your Honour, and I make it a rule to pay for everything I eat.'

TEACHER: 'Are you good at arithmetic?'
PUPIL: 'Yes and no.'
TEACHER: 'What on earth do you mean?'
PUPIL: 'Yes, I'm no good at arithmetic.'

'My youngest boy is troubled with rheumatism.'
'That's bad - how did he get it?'
'He didn't get it - he can't spell it.'

'Did any of your family ever make a brilliant marriage?'
'Only my wife.'

GUEST: 'Does the water always come through the roof like that?'
HOTEL MANAGER: 'No, sir, only when it rains.'

PATIENT: 'Doctor, will I be able to play the violin when my hand is healed?'
DOCTOR: 'Yes, certainly.'
PATIENT: 'That's good – I never could before.'

A farmer's pig was knocked over by a motorist and killed. 'Don't worry,' said the motorist. 'I'll replace your pig.'
'You can't,' roared the farmer, 'you're not fat enough!'

LITTLE BETTY: 'How long is it to my birthday, Mummy?'
MOTHER: 'Oh not long now, dear.'
BETTY: 'Well, is it time for me to begin being good?'

'Did you have any difficulty with your Italian in Rome?'
'No, but the Italians did.'

MUSEUM CURATOR: 'Please be careful of that vase. It's 2,000 years old.'
MOVING-MAN: 'Sure I will, sir, I'll be as careful as if it were new.'

'What have you done to your face?'
'I had a little argument with a bloke about the traffic.'
'Why didn't you call a policeman?'
'He WAS a policeman.'

The office manager pointed to a cigarette butt on his office floor.
'Is this yours, Carruthers?' he said sternly.
'Oh, not at all, sir,' said Carruthers, 'you saw it first.'

INDIGNANT MOTORIST: 'I had the right of way when this man ran straight into me, officer, and yet you say I was responsible. How do you account for that?'
POLICE OFFICER: 'His father is the mayor, his brother is the chief constable, and I'm engaged to his sister.'

FATHER: 'You're always wishing for something you haven't got.'
SON: 'Well, what else can one wish for?'

GERTIE: 'This match won't light.'
BERTIE: 'It did a minute ago when I tried it.'

Man on telephone to fire chief: 'You can't possibly mistake it - it's the only burning house on the street.'

'Did anybody drop a roll of money with a rubber band round it?' asked the man in the bank.
'Yes, I did,' piped up several voices.
'Well, I just found the rubber band,' said the man.

A young lady came to the doctor in distress. 'I've broken my glasses. Do I have to be examined all over again?'
'No,' said the doctor, 'just your eyes.'

'Are your fish fresh?' asked the customer.
'Of course they're fresh madam,' said the fishmonger.
Then, turning round to the slab, 'Keep still, can't you!'

'What's your name?' the policeman asked the Irish driver.
'It's on the side of me van, Officer.'
'It's obliterated.'
'Oh no, sorry, Officer, it's O'Reilly.'

Old Lady (seeing tug-of-war for the first time): 'Wouldn't it be simpler if they got a knife and cut it?'

CUSTOMER: 'Waiter, I can't eat this soup.'
WAITER: 'I'll get the manager, sir.'
CUSTOMER: 'Manager, I can't eat this soup.'
MANAGER: 'Sorry, sir. I'll get the chef.'
CUSTOMER: 'Chef, I can't eat this soup.'
CHEF: 'What's wrong with it?'
CUSTOMER: 'Nothing - I haven't got a spoon.'

Lady to new cleaner: 'Mrs Briggs, did you sweep behind that door?'
Mrs Briggs: 'Oh yes, ma'am - I sweep everything behind the door.'

MOTHER: 'Have you given the goldfish fresh water?'
WILLY: 'No – they haven't drunk all their old water yet.'

SUE: 'What kind of husband would you advise me to take?'
BERYL: 'Take a single man and leave the husbands alone.'

LITTLE WINNIE: 'How much a pound do people pay for babies?'
MOTHER: 'Babies aren't bought by the pound, dear.'
WINNIE: 'Then why do they always weigh them as soon as they're born?'

EMMA: 'Mummy, Jimmy broke my doll.'
MOTHER: 'Oh the naughty boy - how did he do that?'
EMMA: 'I hit him on the head with it.'

MR SHOW-OFF: 'Have you ever hunted bear?'
MR BLOGGS: 'No, but I've hunted in my shorts.'

MRS PROUD: 'My son has been playing the violin for five years.'
FRIEND: 'Dear me, his arms must be very tired.'

Customer at hardware store: 'Who's in charge of the nuts here?'
Assistant: 'Just a moment sir, and I'll take care of you.'

TEACHER: Did your father help you with this arithmetic?
BRIAN: No, Miss, I got it wrong all by myself.

DAN: 'My mother thinks I'm too thin.'
TOM: 'What makes you say that?'
DAN: 'She says she can see right through me.'

DOLLY: 'My mother can play the piano by ear.'
BILLY: 'That's nothing - my dad can fiddle with his moustache.'

Little Suzie had been in the sun and was peeling badly. She ran to her grannie, saying 'Look, grannie, only four years old and I'm wearing out already.'

CONFUCIUS HE SAY

'Confucius, he say ...'

You've probably heard people tell jokes that begin like this. Confucius was in fact a real person - a Chinese thinker who lived fifteen hundred years ago. His wisdom was considered to be very great, though his sayings seemed - at first glance - very straightforward. They seemed so simple when translated into English that some people made fun of them by taking up the line 'Confucius, he say ...' and making jokes. These jokes started off as folksy sayings, and there's usually half of the old saying left. Have a look at the ones below. You should be able to make some up, too - just take a popular saying, such as 'Look after the pennies, and the pounds will look after themselves' and give it the Confucius treatment!

A friend in need is a big nuisance.

He who laughs last doesn't get the joke.

You can fool some of the people all of the time, and all of the people some of the time - but for the rest of the time they will make fools of themselves.

To err is human - so is covering it up.

No legs are so short that they won't reach the ground.

It is better to have loved a short girl than never to have loved a tall.

No artist is so bad that he can't draw his breath.

Do unto others before they do unto you.

Better to keep your mouth shut and have people wonder if you're stupid than to open it and remove all doubt.

Life's like a shower – one wrong turn and you're in hot water.

Early to bed and early to rise means you never see anyone else.

An apple a day keeps the doctor away – if it's thrown in the right direction.

The early bird catches the worm – but who eats worms, anyway?

STRANGE DEFINITIONS

Dictionaries are not usually very funny things, but then, they're not meant to be. However, they are useful if you want to find words for Strange Definitions.

All you do is take an everyday word and give it a funny new meaning. So, if you have 'carpet' you might find the Strange Definition, 'a hamster in a car'! Or perhaps 'slate' which means 'it isn't early' (it's late!.)

Here are some more. You'll soon get the idea and be able to make up your own:

LAZYBONES   A skeleton that doesn't like work.

OUT OF BOUNDS   A kangaroo suffering from exhaustion.

HALFWIT   Somebody who's funny half the time.

FREE SPEECH   Using someone else's phone.

DOCTOR   A person with inside information.

JET-SETTER   A fast-flying dog.

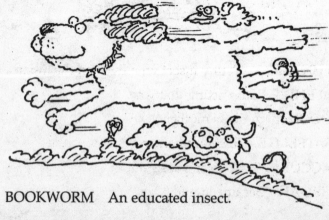

BOOKWORM   An educated insect.

SEASICKNESS   What a doctor does all day.

UNDERCOVER AGENT   A spy in bed.

WATERMELON   A fruit that you can eat, drink and wash your ears with at the same time.

WHOLESOME   The only thing from which you can take the whole and still have some left.

CABARET   A row of taxis.

RHEUMATIC   An apartment at the top of a house.

WORSHIP   A battlecruiser belonging to the Mayor.

DISCOVER   Case for a gramophone record.

DATA   Make an appointment with a lady.

CONVERSION TABLE   A piece of furniture that folds up into something else.

MISINFORM   A schoolgirl.

DECORATION   A speech on board ship.

LUNATIC   A tiny insect who lives on the moon.

BEEHIVE   Stop acting that way.

DOGMA   A dog's mother.

SATELLITE   To commit arson.

ACCURATE   A vicar's assistant.

GROAN   Became larger.

ENTERTAINMENT

Here we have some great ideas for entertaining
your family and friends. You might like to set up a
small stage - or at least have a space surrounded by
chairs where you can try these out.

MUSIC

For a very easy and amusing concert you can play
musical glasses. Fill eight glasses with water. Tip
out some of the water from each glass and then tap
each with the handle of a wooden spoon. You
should get each one to play a different note. When
you've done this, try playing a simple tune such as
'Three Blind Mice'. To add to the fun of the
performance, have a whistle in your mouth, and a
saucepan lid to bash every now and then. The
results may not be great music, but they should be
great fun!

MAGIC

To be funny at magic is quite tricky! The best way is
to learn some simple tricks from a book of magic
and then, when you 'perform' them, pretend to be
very clumsy and do everything wrong. There are
lots of things that will look funny on stage: tripping
over and dropping your pack of cards; having a
goldfish bowl full of water for a trick and then
dropping coins, or buttons into it by mistake;
wearing big braces that get caught up in your
magic wand. One accident should follow another
until, just when everyone is in stitches, you do the
trick properly so the performance comes to a neat
end.

VENTRILOQUISM

Again - do it wrong! To be a good ventriloquist takes many years of training, but to be a bad funny one takes only a few minutes.

Unless you're very lucky, you won't be able to use a proper dummy, but you can make one from an old sock and two round sticky labels. Put the sock on your right hand and push a bit of it between your thumb and forefinger to make a mouth. Peel the two labels off their backing and stick them on above the mouth. You now have your dummy! You can move your thumb about to give the impression that the dummy is speaking, but the funniest bit will be what you say to each other. You must try to do the dummy's lines without moving your lips and without laughing, but exaggerate the difficulties of making the dummy sound normal, and bring in lots of misunderstandings. For example:

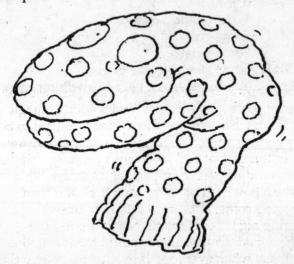

DUMMY: It's windy today isn't it?
YOU: No, it's Thursday, I think.
DUMMY: No, no. Windy. WINDY.
YOU: I'm sure it's Thursday.
DUMMY: Oh! So am I - what have you got to drink?
YOU: What would you like?
DUMMY: Some geer.
YOU: Some what?
DUMMY: Some geer. A gottle of geer.
YOU: You mean, some beer. Why didn't you say 'beer' instead of 'geer'?
DUMMY: I can't say 'guh'.
YOU: You mean 'buh'.
DUMMY: That's right, 'guh'.
YOU: Well, you'll have to do the best you can. Would you like a big bottle of beer or a small one?
DUMMY: I'd like a gig gottle of geer.
YOU: What?
DUMMY: A small one.

And so on!

24

FORTUNE-TELLING FUN

Fortune-telling can be fun. Of course, no one
actually believes in all that stuff. Only this morning
I met a gypsy who told me I was going to have an
accident and …

AAAAAAaaargh!!!!

(NORMAL SERVICE WILL BE RESUMED AS
SOON AS POSSIBLE. DO NOT ADJUST YOUR
BOOK! We will be with you again just as soon as
we have pulled the author out from under the
chandelier …)

Where was I? Oh, yes. I was about to say that fortune-telling is a very serious business. It's not something to be trifled with or made fun of. So, why don't you take a rest from all this being funny business for a while and be Deadly Serious and learn to become a Fortune-Teller? To help you, we have produced a script. This is to give you an idea of what to do.

THE CRYSTAL BALL
Act One Scene One

Scene: The village fete on the green at Long Dangley, a lovely old village in Sussex. The place is a dark tent. Enter you, wearing long dangly earrings, long dangly ringlets, long dangly teeth, a long dangly black shawl, and long dangly green fingernails. Enter your first victim, sorry, your first client, MISS EDITH GREENFLY-CYCLECLIPS, the champion plum-bottling churchwarden of Long Dangley.

YOU: Come in, my dear, and sit down. I see you are troubled ... or was it too much ginger beer in the Refreshment Tent?

MISS E: Are you really Gypsy Rose O'Beans?

YOU: I am indeed she. Sit down, my dear, and take the weight off your plates. That's plates of meat, I mean. Feet. Never mind, dear, just sit down.

MISS E: Can you see into the future?

YOU: If you cross my palm with paper, I can. Especially if it's a five pound note - I can see very well then.

    [MISS E gives you a fiver]

YOU: I shall gaze into my crystal ball. What do you wish to know?

MISS E: Can you see what's going to happen next year at the Long Dangley Plum-Bottling Championships?

YOU: I see mists. And more mists. And more mists. And a dark man ... it's Michael Fish. It must be the weather forecast. Ah, now the mists are clearing. I can see something else. It's a man. A man coming towards you.

MISS E: [shrieks] A man?

YOU: Yes, I see a long dangly man. I mean, a man from Long Dangley. He's tall, dark and ugly ... it's the vicar!

MISS E: [shrieks again] The vicar!!

YOU: Yes. He's judging the plum-bottling. He's come to your plums now. He's tasting them.

MISS E: [further shrieks] Have I won?

YOU: He's passing on ... he's talking to a man dressed in a tablecloth ... he's an Arab. He's won! Yes, he's won! He's a Sheik!

MISS E: [shrieks] A Sheik!

YOU: He's won it. He's won it with his jar of pickled sheep's ears!

[MISS E *flounces out in a huff, which was knitted for her by her aged aunt,* LADY KNITS-BADDLEY *of Lacey Pullovers, Dorset.*]

Tea and Tarot
Act One Scene Two

Scene: A dismal tea-room. The waitress, tables, chairs and cake-trolley are covered in cobwebs. The clock stopped in 1938 and the service a long time before that. Into this gloomy scene steps ... fresh-faced Health Food fanatic and Vegetarian MISS TRISHIA NUTTER. *In the corner of the tea-shoppe, amongst the cobwebs ... something stirs ... yes! It's* YOU!

YOU: I can see by your eyes that you have
    trouble ahead.
MISS N: A glass of apple juice and two prune
    cookies, please.
YOU: I told you so.
MISS N: Are you the waitress?
YOU: No, I'll call her. Waitress! Two teas and a
    Tarot pack, please. No, my dear, I'm the Reader
    in Tea Leaves. One glance into your cup and I
    can see what's in store for you.
MISS N: Really? How super! O.K. then!
    [*She drinks her tea*].
YOU: [*chanting magically*]:
    Abracadabra, and Sneezlegum,
    Toasted tea-cakes and brownies -
    The tea-leaves that have touched your lips
    Will now reveal your future.
MISS N: But it doesn't rhyme!
YOU: Rhyming's extra. Aha! I see something
    terrible in store for you.
MISS N: Wh-What is it?
YOU: A leg of lamb.
MISS N: A leg of lamb?
YOU: Yes, yes. A leg of lamb, and it will do you
    great harm.
MISS N: Never! I will not let it pass my lips! I shall
    never eat a leg of lamb again!
YOU: That won't matter, it's going to fall on
    your head and ...
              AAAAAAAAAARGH!!!!
    [*Unfortunately, and unpredictably, your chair collapses,
    and you have to end the Fortune-Telling for the day*].

              CURTAIN

YOUR OWN FORTUNE-TELLING FUN

In olden times, people tried to forecast the future in some very odd ways. The Ancient Greeks had something called the Oracle. This was a voice that lived in a cave. It spoke only if presents were brought, so it was quite a clever voice. No one ever saw the owner of the voice. It was a very well-kept secret.

There aren't many Oracles about today - not ones that live in caves, anyway. You could have one, although it would have to live in a cellar or a cupboard and not a cave, and it wouldn't be just a voice - it would be you! Invite your friends to question the Oracle about very important things, such as:

'What's for tea today?'
                or:
'Who's going to win the Cup?'

You, the Oracle, should be hidden so that you can be heard but not seen. When you are asked a question you should have some special way of answering. For example, the answers to the second question above might be:

When moons go green from too much pop!
    When chips fry on the grill!
Then EVERTON will win the Cup,
    But Arsenal never will!

Your friends will either storm your 'cave' or shout out, 'WHAT??!' If so, you should call out quickly, '3–1'.

There are, of course, the trusty old tea-leaves. When you pour your tea, don't strain it! Drink as much as you possibly can, then chuck away the rest of the tea. There should be tea-leaves left at the bottom of the cup. If you look at them for a while you should be able to see something - a ship (which might mean you're going on a long journey), or a bicycle (which might mean you're going on a short one). You might see anything, but if there's nothing there at all, it means either that the future is very blank, or your mother's using tea-bags to make the tea!

FUNNY GAMES

Another way to entertain your friends is to show them
how to play Funny Games. You must be sure about
how the games are played, though. You won't be very
popular if you begin a game which you can't finish.
Go through these games first just to make sure you
will be able to explain to others how to play them.

THE PICTURE FRAME GAME

This rib-tickling game is nice and simple. Just find
an old picture frame and with your friends
watching you, hold it in front of your face so that
you're framed! You mustn't laugh or even smile,
because you're supposed to be like one of those
serious portraits you see in art galleries. The more
serious you look, the more your friends will laugh;
but then, if you laugh too, ask one of them to try it
and see if he can do better!

THE LAUGHING GAME

This is another simple game, in which you have to
choose a victim. Once you've got one, tell him he
has to look stern even though you're all going to try
to make him laugh. This can be done in any way -
by making funny noises, or strange faces. If he does
laugh, someone else must take his place.

FAMILIAR FACES

This calls for a little bit of preparation. Look in newspapers or magazines for familiar faces wearing funny expressions. Cut them out and stick them on a big sheet. Give each a number. Your friends then try to guess the names. They might recognise Princess Anne in an ordinary photograph but will they know her when she's eating sour fruit? You can have pictures of famous football players, or cricketers, or television people, or politicians - of anybody at all, as long as they all have funny looks on their faces.

BITE THE PENNY

This is a messy game so put a large sheet, or several pieces of newspaper on the floor. Fill a large, shallow bowl half-full with flour. Then bury about half a dozen washed, dry pennies in the flour. (Make sure they are really dry or the flour will get gluey.) The unfortunate penny-biter must now get the pennies out of the flour using his teeth, but nothing else. (When it comes to your turn, the knack is to blow away the flour until the penny can be picked up easily. Don't dive in!)

ANKLE GUESSING

Get some of your friends to lie on the floor, and
cover them with a sheet, leaving only their bare feet
sticking out. Give the rest paper and pencils, and
going from left to right, get them to write down
who the feet belong to.

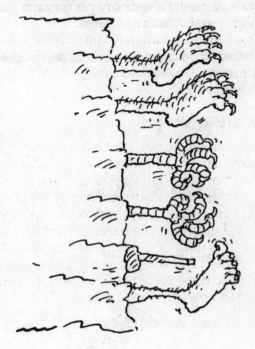

CROSSBREEDS

This is a good game for two people. Draw the top
half of a person or animal, and then fold the paper
over so that only a very small amount shows. Next
your friend draws a bottom half on to your
drawing - and you do the same for hers. Then you
unfold both drawings and have a good laugh at the
strange sort of animals you've created!

LAST WILL AND TESTAMENT

This game can be quite hilarious - you have freedom to choose your beneficiaries* and your bequests** but you don't know what you are bequeathing - until later.

You will need a sheet of paper for each person playing, marked out as follows:

I, being of unsound mind do hereby will and bequeath:
1. my
    to
    so that (s)he will

2. my
    to
    in the hope that (s)he will

3. my
    to
    and ask that (s)he will

4. my
    to
    on condition that (s)he will

*Beneficiaries are the people to whom you leave your possessions in your will.

**Your bequests are what you leave them.

The space after 'my' you leave blank but after the word 'to' you write the name of the beneficiary (this can be a friend, a television personality, or even Battersea Dogs Home).

On the last line write the reason for the bequest, i.e., 'So she can keep warm in the long winter evenings', or 'In the hope that it will keep him in at nights'.

When the forms have been completed each person is given a list of bequests and inserts one after the word 'my' in each case.

Then you read out your own will!

Some sample bequests:

Empty yoghurt carton	Roller boot
Old toothbrush	Athlete's foot
Garden gnome	Dustbin lid
Join-the-dots book	Bart Simpson badge
Dead goldfish	Apple core
Chipped mug	Wine gums
Old trainer	Broken zip
Gumball	Frog spawn
Macaroni	Scratched CD
Old school tie	Smelly football socks
Cockroach collection	Old train ticket
Slice of stale bread	Irish penny
Completed crossword puzzle	Stale fish finger
Lollipop stick	Banana skin
Catfood	Breath freshener
Soggy cornflakes	One holey glove
Gorgonzola cheese	Jacket button
Library ticket	Coca-Cola can
String vest	Safety pin
Picture of Queen Victoria	Broken lightbulb
Used tea bag	Stained beer mat
Olive oil	Dracula outfit

FRONT PAGE NEWS

When there's important news, the newspapers will keep some space free on the front page and fill it in at the last moment with all the latest details. Because they are in a hurry, misprints and misunderstandings occur. Here are some real examples. If you look closely at your newspapers you might spot some gems like these. Collect them in a scrapbook so you can make your friends laugh on rainy days.

On board the train, trapped by falls of earth at Wilmington, were $1^1/2$ passengers, mostly female.

NEW COUNCIL SETTLES DOWN WELL

One of the newer M.P.s rushed across the floor to shake a clenched fish in the Prime Minister's face.

PENGUIN TO PROTEST AT
ANTARCTIC TALKS

Ice-cream vendors, expecting big earnings in the next few days, have arranged for huge socks to supply the city.

SHEILA IS THE FIRST LADY TO TAKE OVER THE TOAST AND MARMALADE SHOW, WHICH HAS ALWAYS BEEN A MALE PRESERVE.

WHEN WASHING WINDOWS, ADD A SMALL AMOUNT OF VINEGAR TO THE WATER. THIS WILL KEEP THE FLIES AWAY AS WELL AS CLEANING THEM.

AN AMERICAN MUSICIAN WAS FOUND IN A DOORWAY HOLDING A HAMMER, SCREWDRIVER AND SPANNER AT 3.00 A.M. HE TOLD POLICE 'I WAS JUST GOING TO MAKE A GUITAR'.

In spite of the snags that bedevil every big exhibition the British Museum's spectacular display of gold and silver dating from ad 300 to 700 opens tomorrow. Preparations for handling crows of Tutankhamun dimensions were well in hand yesterday.

THIS IS A QUIET NEIGHBOURHOOD WITH
DOGS AND CHILDREN RIDING BICYCLES.

Not all of the cars recalled had defects. For instance,
General Motors recalled 32,640 Buicks, Oldsmobiles
and Pontiacs to find 1,250 which had been fitted
with wheels.

WILL LADIES KINDLY EMPTY TEAPOTS, RINSE
ROUND, AND, BEFORE LEAVING, PLEASE
STAND UPSIDE DOWN IN THE SINK.

Notice is given fixing the charge for the use of the
WC at the zoo in the Bois de Vincennes at 3 francs.
This new tariff will take effect retrospectively as
from 1 July last.

The seats in the vicinity of the bandstand are for the
use of ladies. Gentlemen should make use of them
only after the former are seated.

IT PAYS TO ADVERTISE!

Advertisements go wrong, too! These odd ads can be put in another part of your scrapbook or you can copy them and put them in a folder. It's a good idea to put down the name of the paper you found them in. This adds interest and can be very funny - there's a paper in Australia called the *Toowoomba Chronicle*!

THE DUN COW REQUIRES FULL TIME SNAKE WAITRESS.

1929 ROLLS ROYCE HEARSE FOR SALE. ORIGINAL BODY.

LOST - BLIMPTON AREA. BLACK LONGHAIRED BUTCHER'S ASSISTANT. IF FOUND WANDERING RING 4925 - REWARD. SENTIMENTAL VALUE ONLY.

DUE TO FALL OUT ACROBAT REQUIRED.

ENTERTAINMENTS – CLOWN JOEY (PLEASE SEE 'DEATHS' COLUMN).

WANTED: GRAND PIANO FOR WOMAN WITH CARVED MAHOGANY LEGS.

BED AND BREAKFAST, REASONABLE RATES, COMFORTABLE BEDS, HOT AND COLD RUNNING WAITER IN EVERY ROOM.

DECORATOR - SPECIALISES IN INFERIOR WORK. IMMEDIATE ATTENTION.

CRASH COURSES ARE AVAILABLE FOR THOSE WISHING TO DRIVE QUICKLY.

INTELLIGENT YOUNG LADY WANTED FOR INTERESTING AND RESPONSIBLE WORK. MUST BE PROPER GOOD AT GRAMMER AND SPELLING.

HELP WANTED: MAN WANTED TO HANDLE DYNAMITE. MUST BE ABLE TO TRAVEL UNEXPECTEDLY.

WOODFORD SOCIETY ANNUAL CHEESE AND WIND PARTY WILL BE HELD NEXT SUNDAY EVENING.

FOR SALE OAK TABLE WITH STRONG LEGS AND VANISHED TOP.

FOR SALE TERRACED HOUSE BRICK BUILT WITH STALE ROOF.

CHARLADY REQUIRED FOR LIGHT HOUSEWORK AND HOVERING.

TUTOR OFFERS O AND A LEVEL POACHING TO EXAM CANDIDATES.

LOVELY HOLIDAY COTTAGE. SLEEPS SIX. ONLY FIFTEEN MILES WALK TO THE SEA.

Beefburger & chips	....	80p
Egg and chips	....	60p
Sausage and beans	....	70p
Children	....	50p

WANTED - SINGLE-HANDED CHEF FOR
LUXURY HOTEL IN LAKE DISTRICT.

RENT A POLAR BEAR CHEAP. EATS ANYTHING.
VERY FOND OF CHILDREN.

AN ENCYCLOPAEDIA OF JOKES

The best funny men have a joke for every occasion -
a story that fits every topic. To help you, we
proudly present our Encyclopaedia of Jokes, an
A–Z of different subjects, each with its own joke.

A

AIRPLANE

Aboard an airplane high over the Atlantic Ocean:
　'Ladies and Gentlemen. This is your Captain
speaking. I've some good news and some bad
news. First, the good news. We have perfect
visibility, clear weather, we're making record time
and we'd be there in half an hour if it weren't for
the bad news which is, we're lost.'

B

BAND

CUSTOMER:　'Will the band play anything I ask
them to?'
WAITER:　'Yes, sir.'
CUSTOMER:　'Well, ask them to play cards.'

C

CAKE

MOTHER: 'Why are you cleaning up the spilt coffee with cake?'
GEORGE: 'Well, Mum, it's sponge cake!'

CANNIBALS

The trouble with cannibal jokes is that they aren't in good taste.

D

DOCTOR

A husband took his wife to the doctor.
HUSBAND: 'Doctor, my wife thinks she's a chicken.'
DOCTOR: 'That's terrible. How long has she been like this?'
HUSBAND: 'Three years.'
DOCTOR: 'Why didn't you bring her to see me sooner?'
HUSBAND: 'We needed the eggs.'

DUCK

JO: 'We went over a duckway last night.'
JILL: 'What's a duckway?'
JO: 'About five pounds.'

E

ELEPHANT

PATIENT: 'Can a person be in love with an elephant?'
DOCTOR: 'No, it's out of the question.'
PATIENT: 'Do you know anyone who wants to buy a very big engagement ring?'

EYES

DOCTOR: 'Have your eyes been checked in the last few months?'
PATIENT: 'No, Doctor. They've always been plain blue.'

F

FISH

What fish has a good ear for music?
A piano-tuna!

FOOT

JAMES: 'I'll never be able to leave you.'
RACHEL: 'Do you like me that much?'
JAMES: 'No. You're standing on my foot.'

G

GRAVES

When an old Red Indian called Short Cake died, his tribe argued about who should dig his grave. In the end, his widow settled it. She said, 'Squaw bury Short Cake.'

H

HAIR

FATHER: 'Oh, dear. I think my hair's getting thinner.'
MOTHER: 'Don't worry - nobody likes fat hair.'

HORSE

The God of Thunder went for a ride on his favourite filly. He cried out, 'I'm Thor!'
The horse said, 'Well, you forgot the thaddle, thilly!'

I

INVISIBLE MAN

NURSE: 'Doctor, doctor. The Invisible Man's here.'
DOCTOR: 'Tell him I can't see him.'

J

JAIL

The sword swallower's in jail again - he hiccupped and stabbed two people.

JUDGE

JUDGE: 'The next person who raises his voice in this court will be thrown out!'
PRISONER: 'Hip, hip hooray!'

46

K

KING KONG

ARTHUR: 'I can trace my ancestors all the way back to royalty.'
BILL: 'King Kong?'

L

LADDER

JUDGE: 'What do you mean by bringing a ladder in here?'
PRISONER: 'I want to take my case to a higher court.'

LOONY
BUS CONDUCTOR: 'Come down, there's no standing on top of this bus.'
LOONY: 'Why not?'
BUS CONDUCTOR: 'It's a single-decker.'

M

MILLIONAIRE

From the will of a miserly millionaire: '... and to my dear nephew whom I promised to remember in my will, "Hello, there, Bill!"'

MUSIC

COMPOSER: 'Why do you play this bit of music over and over?'
PIANIST: 'It haunts me.'
COMPOSER: 'I'm not surprised. You've murdered it often enough.'

N

NAILS

'At last I've been able to make my son stop biting his nails.'
'How did you do it?'
'I made him wear shoes.'

O

ONIONS

JIM: 'Did you hear about the man who lived on onions alone?'
JACK: 'No, but anyone who does ought to live alone!'

OPERATIONS

SURGEON: 'How is the patient feeling after his operation?'
NURSE: 'Fine, except that we can hear a double heartbeat.'
SURGEON: 'Oh, so that's where my wristwatch went!'

P

PIANO TUNER

PUZZLED MAN: 'I didn't call for a piano tuner.'
PIANO TUNER: 'No, it was your neighbours who sent for me.'

POISON

Did you hear what happened to the scientist who mixed poison ivy and a four-leaf clover?
He had a rash of good luck.

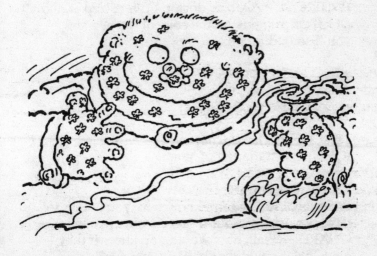

Q

QUESTIONS

What has never asked a question, but still gets plenty of answers?

A doorbell!

R

RESTAURANT

FIRST TRAMP: 'I know a restaurant where we can eat dirt cheap.'
SECOND TRAMP: 'I don't like dirt!'

S

SLEEP

PATIENT: 'Doctor, doctor, I can't sleep at night.'
DOCTOR: 'Lie on the edge of the bed and you'll soon drop off.'

T

TEACHER

TEACHER: 'John, what comes after the letter "A"?'
JOHN: 'All the rest of 'em.'

TRAIN

PASSENGER: 'I don't know why you bother to have timetables - your trains are always late.'
GUARD: 'Well, how would you know if they were late if you didn't have a timetable?'

U

UMBRELLA

JIM: 'When should a mouse carry an umbrella?'
JACK:'When it's raining cats and dogs.'

UNDERWEAR

TONY: 'Are there any holes in your underwear?'
MIKE: 'How rude! Of course there aren't.'
TONY: 'Well, how do you get your feet through?!'

V

VEGETARIANS

Once upon a time there was a tribe of vegetarian cannibals. They were very fussy. They would only eat Swedes.

W

WAITER

CUSTOMER: 'Waiter, do you have frogs' legs?'
WAITER: 'Of course, sir.'
CUSTOMER: 'Then leap over the counter and get me a drink.'

WEREWOLF

GEORGE: 'Mummy, Mummy, all the kids say I look like a werewolf!'
MUMMY: 'Shut up, George, and comb your face.'

X

XMAS

FRED: 'What did the fireman's wife find in her stocking at Christmas?'
BERT: 'A ladder!'

X-RAY

PATIENT: 'What does the X-ray of my head show?'
DOCTOR: 'Nothing.'

Y

YELLOW

DAN: 'What's yellow on the inside but green on the outside?'
GRAN: 'A banana disguised as a cucumber.'

Z

ZOO

What do you get if you cross an elephant with a goldfish?
Swimming trunks!

KNOCK-KNOCKS

People have been having fun with Knock-Knock
jokes for over half a century. Over the next fifty
years you can make your family and friends laugh
by trying out *your* Knock-Knock jokes on them.
Here are some examples to inspire you.

Knock, knock.
Who's there?
Lion.
Lion who?
Lion here on your doorstep. Open up.

Knock, knock.
Who's there?
Lydia.
Lydia who?
Lydia teapot.

Knock, knock.
Who's there?
Eileen.
Eileen who?
Eileen'd on the fence and it broke.

Knock, knock.
Who's there?
Norma Lee.
Norma Lee who?
Norma Lee I wouldn't trouble you but I need help.

Knock, knock.
Who's there?
Esther.
Esther who?
Esther anything I can do for you?

Knock, knock.
Who's there?
Thea.
Thea who?
Thea later, alligator.

Knock, knock.
Who's there?
Sonia.
Sonia who?
Sonia bird in a gilded cage.

Knock, knock.
Who's there?
Jester.
Jester who?
Jester song at twilight.

Knock, knock.
Who's there?
Sacha.
Sacha who?
Sacha lot o' questions ...

Knock, knock.
Who's there?
Theresa.
Theresa who?
Theresa Green.

Knock, knock.
Who's there?
Eddie.
Eddie who?
Eddieboddy in there?

Knock, knock.
Who's there?
Sharon.
Sharon who?
Sharon share alike.

Knock, knock.
Who's there?
Watson.
Watson who?
Watson your mind?

Knock, knock.
Who's there?
Arthur.
Arthur who?
Arthur any more at home like you?

Knock, knock.
Who's there?
Señor.
Señor who?
Señor mother out and let me in.

Knock, knock.
Who's there?
Bernardette.
Bernardette who?
Bernardette all my dinner and I'm starving.

Knock, knock.
Who's there?
Lionel.
Lionel who?
Lionel get you nowhere - better spill the beans.

Knock, knock.
Who's there?
Juno.
Juno who?
Juno what time it is?

SHAGGY DOG STORIES

Long Jokes are called Shaggy Dog stories. This may be because Shaggy Dogs have long coats, or perhaps ... well, it doesn't matter. The thing is that long stories are not only more difficult to remember, but they're much more difficult to tell than short ones. Your audience will quickly get bored unless there's something funny at the beginning. So, it's best to choose stories that have funny or odd subjects, like the one about the gorilla in a coffee shop. This way the audience will wonder what the punch line is going to be, so you'll keep their attention until the end. That is, as long as you memorise the joke well - and don't fluff it! If your Shaggy Dog story is met by a great groan or, worse, a stony silence, it is best to follow it straightaway with some jokes from the 'Quick Quips' section!

THE GORILLA JOKE

A gorilla went into a coffee shop, sat down and ordered a coffee. The waiter was a bit nervous at first, but there weren't any other customers and the gorilla seemed quite friendly, so he let him sit in peace. Who'd argue with a gorilla, anyway?

While the waiter made the coffee, he watched the gorilla from the kitchen. The gorilla just sat there, staring at the ceiling. The kettle boiled and the waiter made a fresh cup of coffee and took it in. The gorilla handed him a five-pound note, and proceeded to drink the coffee. The waiter took the five-pound note and went back to the kitchen to get some change. While he was there he watched the gorilla, who drank the coffee, but for the rest of the time just stared at the ceiling. The waiter thought to himself, 'That gorilla won't know the difference between a pound note and a five-pound note - he's only a gorilla, after all ...' So he took a pound coin and went in to give it to the gorilla. As he handed it over, he said:

'We don't get many gorillas in here.'

The gorilla took the pound coin and replied:

'I'm not surprised, with coffee at four pounds a cup.'

MAKE-UP FUN

It can be great fun to make-up and dress up - and it's another excellent way of being funny. Remember to ask before using any of the bits and pieces lying round the house. If you don't, and they turn out to be priceless, you could be in real trouble. You'd need more than this book to make your parents laugh if you cut up your grandmother's silk scarf to make Lawrence of Arabia's head-gear!

DRESSING-UP

If you look through all the old cupboard, wardrobes and attics in your house, you're bound to find lots of things you can use to dress up in. Here's a list of people you can dress up as:

LAWRENCE OF ARABIA - an old dressing-gown, a tea towel for your head-dress, kept in place by a dressing-gown cord or a tie.

DRACULA - a dark blanket for a cloak, black suit or jersey and trousers underneath. Make yourself some fangs out of cardboard.

A GHOST - you should be able to find an old white sheet or table-cloth, and if it's really old, ask if you can paint a ghastly, staring face onto it.

MAKE-UP

Dressing up and parading around is terrific fun.
But why not do the thing properly and try make-
up, too? Ask your mum or sister if you can use
some of theirs. There are lots of weird and
wonderful things you can do with make-up. Here
are a couple of sample make-up plans:

A COMEDY SHOW

Now you've got the hang of costume and make-up,
why don't you go the whole hog and put on a
comedy show for your friends and family? Get
together and plan it with a few other people. Try
and keep it full of short bits, not a long-drawn-out
play - just in case things go wrong! It's easier to
give up a little sketch and race on to the next, rather
than try and rescue a long and involved play that's
gone wrong. Short sketches are much funnier, too!

One of the acts could be a stand-up comic who simply came on and told jokes. But it would be a lot funnier if you did it in some kind of costume - say, a clown (pyjamas and clown make-up) or even Superman!

As another act, you could perform little sketches with two or three other people. Use some of the jokes in this book. Or act out some charades - you'll find some suggestions for animal ones in the 'Animal Magic' section on page 105. If you think ahead and plan them carefully, you can make them really funny!

Just a word of warning. Don't be so keen on the idea of dressing-up that you plan a show full of too many weird and wonderful costumes. Remember that changing into costumes takes absolutely ages, and you don't want to keep your audience waiting - even if it's only Mum and Dad dozing on the sofa! Have a fantastic costume of course, but wear it throughout or plan carefully how to have time to change out of it if you need to. Waiting for performers who are taking ages changing can be very boring!

If the audience have enjoyed themselves, they may want to give you a bit of extra pocket-money as a token of appreciation - if so, why not give it to a charity? In fact, you could make Christmas happier for lots of people by doing a series of these comedy shows in your friends' houses, collecting for Oxfam or Save the Children. Why not? After all, being funny can spread happiness in all sorts of ways!

NUTS IN MAY

You can be Nutty in May - or June - or July, or in any month for that matter! Especially April, when it's April Fool's Day!

Make people laugh by doing nutty things; balancing an eel on the end of your nose isn't easy - but mastering a Funny Walk is.

Here are some suggestions for ways to be nutty all the year round.

FUNNY WALKING

You've probably seen Charlie Chaplin walking his funny walk - a sort of side to side movement made funnier because his shoes are so big and awkward to manage. Your funny walk can be 'aided' by a pair of your father's shoes - if you can walk safely in them. Carry a walking-stick, or pretend to carry a tray of tea-cups. Let your legs go wild when you walk - swing each leg as far backwards and forwards as it will go without you losing your balance. Try to make each step the same - that is, make each leg do the same things every time you take a step.

BARMY NOISES

Get a friend to play the Barmy Noises game with you. One of you has to think of some very unlikely thing, and the other has to illustrate it without any outside help.

The sort of thing for which you have to make the right noises could be the sound of a sockful of custard being blown through a wind tunnel and hitting a cow.

WELLY-THROWING

Lots of nuts throw wellies. They throw them at teapots, or trees, or over hurdles made of bits of rope. Often nuts just see how far they can throw a welly, so if you want to see who the champion well-thrower is among your friends, find one or two Wellington boots and a few markers, and go to a place where there's some room. BUT do watch out for old ladies, and anyone else who might not appreciate being hit by a lot of nuts in May - or June, or whenever you decide to do it.

SILLY HIDE-AND-SEEK

To make your friends think you've gone completely mad, get them to play this cranky game. You should have some odd objects which can be tied or pinned to you - things like a dandelion, or a vest or a tea strainer. Hide one somewhere in the house. The person who finds it has to shout 'SILLY' and pin the object onto his or her body. While everyone else counts to twenty, this person then hides the next odd object and waits while the others search for it. Those with objects on them should do their waiting out in the front garden where everyone can see them!

LEFT ON THE SHELF

Those books on your shelf - are you fed up with looking at them, and wondering why they don't seem funnier, or more useful? Perhaps it's just that you never find one you want to read? Well, you can brighten things up if you write your own books instead of reading other people's. Just get all those jokes you have collected and try to put them into sections: that is, see if they're 'Animal Jokes' or 'Ghost Jokes', etc. When you've got enough of each sort you can put them into a bigger book and arrange them in alphabetical order. For example - Animals, Cannibals, Cars, Doctors, Ghosts, Monsters, Teachers, Waiters. If all this seems too much trouble, just put them all in a big book, and give it a funny title. Your title can suit the sort of jokes in the book or just be silly, like all the others below. If you get enough titles you can even have a book of them and give it a title:

HOW TO BE FUNNY *by Jess Joe King*

NAPOLEON'S ONLY DEFEAT *by Peter Retreat*

HOW TO KEEP THE RAIN OUT *by Anna Rack*

PREPARE TO REPENT *by Celeste Chance*

HOW TO APOLOGISE *by Thayer Thorry*

WHAT'S UP, DOC? *by Howie Dewin*

ARITHMETIC SIMPLIFIED *by Lois Carmen Denominator*

WHO KILLED CAIN? *by Howard I. Know*

EARLY RISER *by R. U. Upjohn*

THE MYSTERY OF THE FRUIT MACHINE *by Jack Potts*

ROUND THE MOUNTAIN *by Sheila B. Cumming*

THE STAFF OF LIFE *by Roland Butter*

HOW TO BECOME AN OXFORD BLUE *by Rowan Daly*

THE MAN WHO COULD WORK MIRACLES *by Betty Cant*

YOU NEED INSURANCE *by Justin Case*

MY LIFE OF CRIME *by Robin Banks*

MY LIFE OF DEBT *by Elwys Owen*

MY DEPARTED LOVER *by Hamish Hugh*

COLOURFUL CARTOONS

Another way of keeping your friends laughing is by drawing clever pictures that tell a joke. They can be like newspaper cartoons, or they can be like the one below, which is an illustration of one of the jokes from the 'Ridiculous Riddles' section.

What bird will never get the vote?

It doesn't matter if you're no good at drawing - just do matchstick-men. You can also draw 'Strange Definitions' pictures. Use one of your own definitions, or find one from the 'Strange Definitions' section and do a picture-joke, like the ones on the next page:

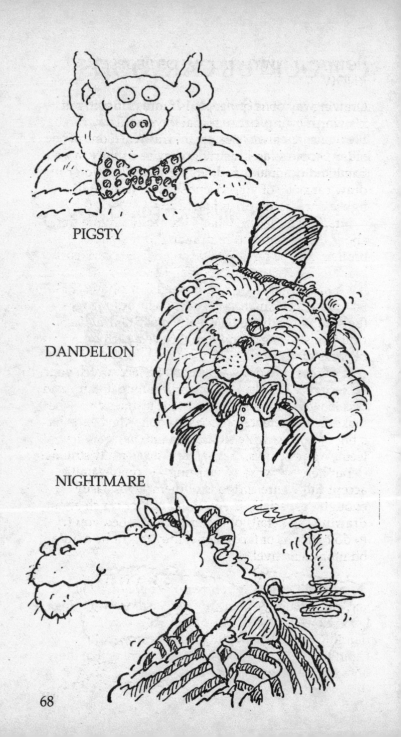

PIGSTY

DANDELION

NIGHTMARE

68

HOW TO DRAW CARTOONS OF PEOPLE YOU KNOW

Drawing cartoons of people is more difficult, but it's worth trying, because it always amuses everyone. It's always easier to draw cartoons of older people's faces, because they're usually more fixed and original than younger faces. But you can draw cartoons of your friends if you draw full-figure ones, rather than just heads.

First, try to decide what's the really unique thing about the person you're drawing. If it's your brother, maybe he has very long legs, or very curly hair, or always wears a football jersey. Or maybe he has a habit, such as biting his nails, or saying 'Er ...' So - draw a pin man, with curly hair or long legs (be sure to make the hair really curly and the legs ridiculously long) - and you'll have a cartoon likeness of him.

If you want to draw a cartoon of a face, watch your subject very closely. Look at your auntie and try and decide what her most characteristic features are - what makes her different from other people. Maybe she has a big nose, or a wide smile, or a gap between her teeth. Whatever it is, exaggerate it so it's really striking.

But here's a word of warning - people usually accept full-figure cartoons of themselves easily enough - especially if you don't bother much about drawing the details of the faces. But when you try to do cartoons of faces alone, they might be a little bit more sensitive!

QUICK QUIPS

You learn those Shaggy Dog Stories for when you had plenty of time to entertain your friends, but there are moments when Quick Quips are the only thing - you can always fit in a few between lessons at school, for instance!

These jokes also come in handy immediately after a long story, or a trick or a game that hasn't worked properly. Or, if you go to the dentist and he's feeling a bit down in the mouth, tell him a few quickies to cheer him up:

See your tailor - and have a fit!

A myth is a lady with a lisp but no husband.

I get on a ferry and every time it makes me cross.

A skeleton is a someone with his outside off.

I'm not saying my cellar's damp, but when I put down a mousetrap I caught a fish!

When I was at school I was teacher's pet. She couldn't afford a dog.

'The refuse-men are here.'
'Tell them we don't need any.'

Advice to worms - sleep late!

'Waiter, bring me some turtle soup - and make it snappy!'

'I don't like cabbage, and I'm glad I don't like it because if I did, I'd eat it - and I hate the stuff!'

A bird in the hand makes it hard to blow your nose.

'I don't care who you are, Fatso - get those reindeer off my roof!'

I say, I say - have you heard about the umbrella salesman who saved his money for a sunny day?

If you show me a thirsty tailor, I'll show you a dry cleaner.

A scrambler's a motorbike that can cook eggs.

If a diver works extra hours, he gets paid undertime.

If a plug doesn't fit - socket!

Baby budgerigars are called budgets.

RIDICULOUS RIDDLES

What is a riddle? The dictionary defines it as a 'conundrum', which is a great help as long as you know what a conundrum is. If you look up 'conundrum', it says 'riddle'!

A riddle is a question with a clever or a witty answer. The question might be:

'Where do all good turkeys
go when they die?'
The witty thinker should reply:
'To oven, of course!'

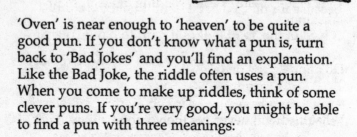

'Oven' is near enough to 'heaven' to be quite a good pun. If you don't know what a pun is, turn back to 'Bad Jokes' and you'll find an explanation. Like the Bad Joke, the riddle often uses a pun. When you come to make up riddles, think of some clever puns. If you're very good, you might be able to find a pun with three meanings:

'What do you call a statue of a soldier with its gun and arms missing?'
And the answer is, "armless!'

He's without his arms, without his gun - also called an 'arm' - and he's harmless without any weapon. You can be just as clever with simpler puns. Have a look at the ones in the riddles on the next few pages and you'll soon get the idea.

What squeals more loudly than a pig with a toothache?
Two pigs with toothache.

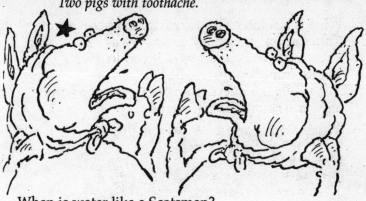

When is water like a Scotsman?
When it's piping hot.
★
What made the Tower of Pisa lean?
It stopped eating spaghetti.
★
Why is it a waste of time sending a telegram to
Washington?
Because he's dead.
★
Do hands grow on trees?
Yes - palm trees.
★
What bird will never get the vote?
A Mynah, because he'll always be too young.
★
Why is a vampire a cheap date?
Because he eats necks to nothing.
★
What's black and white and red all over?
Am embarrassed zebra.
★
What did the Mona Lisa say to the gallery attendant?
I've been framed.

What dance do tin-openers do?
> *The Can-Can.*

★

Why didn't the little pigs listen to their dad?
> *Because he was a boar.*

★

What's got teeth but can't bite?
> *A comb.*

★

What did the cannibal have for supper?
> *Baked beings on toast.*

What hangs in a fruit tree and shouts for help?
> *A damson in distress.*

★

What's the best thing to do with a blue apple?
> *Cheer it up.*

★

What is the cheapest way to get to China?
> *Be born there.*

What can you put in a glass but not take out of it?
A crack.

★

What is a volcano?
A mountain with hiccups.

★

What grows up and grows down at the same time?
A baby duckling.

★

What did the old man do when he thought he was
dying?
Went and sat in the living room.

★

What did one strawberry say to the other strawberry?
'If it wasn't for you we wouldn't be in this jam.'

★

Is it best to write on an empty or a full stomach?
Neither - it's best to use paper.

★

Why was the insect kicked out of the forest?
Because it was a litterbug.

★

What is a fast duck?
A quick quack.

What do you call a magician with a helicopter?
A flying saucerer.

★

Why are sheep always short of money?
Because they're always being fleeced.

★

Why couldn't the dog catch his tail?
Because it is hard to make ends meet these days.

★

What has four fingers and a thumb but is not a hand?
A glove.

SIGNS OF THE TIMES

Watch out for funny signs! They're everywhere, and looking out for them can shorted a long car journey. Persuade your parents to give a prize for the funniest sign, and, if you can manage to, write down all the good ones so that you can add them to your books of jokes when you get back home. The signs may be funny on their own, or they may be funny because of their position. For example someone passed a pub recently which was called The Omnibus Inn. It had a sign outside which said 'NO COACHES'!

Here are some other examples:

DUE TO A STRIKE, GRAVEDIGGING WILL BE DONE BY A SKELETON CREW

Horse Manure
A filled bag, 25p
Do it yourself, 15p

DANCE, DISCOTHEQUE
Highly Exclusive
ALL WELCOME

BRING YOUR LUGGAGE TO US -
WE WILL SEND IT IN ALL DIRECTIONS

LADIES MAY HAVE FITS UPSTAIRS

HOLES PAINTED WHITE NOT TO BE DUG

CUSTOMERS WHO FIND OUR STAFF RUDE SHOULD WAIT AND SEE THE MANAGER

PLEASE IN CASE OF FIRE DO YOUR BEST TO ALARM THE HALL PORTER

PIERCED EARS - £2.00 a pair

BEWARE OF
TRAINS
GOING
BOTH WAYS
AT ONCE

CATTLE PLEASE
CLOSE GATE

DUN-ROMIN

A SENSE OF TRADITION

On a rainy day, why not invent some traditions?
This may sound impossible, but if you think of some
real traditions like the Changing of the Guard, or
the tradition of ducking people in the village pond
at certain times of the year, or beating the parish
boundary, you will probably be able to come up
with your own. There's no need for the ceremony
to mean anything, though it's fun inventing reasons
for each odd action.

Here are a couple to give you the idea. You are
advised NOT to try them out!

HATNIP-CHUCKING

This age-old tradition has been handed down from
father to son, and handed back up again when the
son found out what a hatnip was. It's a cross
between a bowler hat and a turnip. The traditional
way of making one is to get a bowler hat and cut it
into little pieces. In the old days these pieces were
mixed with brown sauce and raddishes. This was
because when food was scarce people ate their
bowler hats rather than go hungry, but they had to
mix the pieces with brown sauce and radishes as
bowler hats really don't taste very good on their own.

After the hat is cut up, the turnip is cut in half
and its centre scooped out. The bowler hat mixture
is put into the scooped-out bits. Then the two
halves of the turnip are put back together, and
stuck up with sticky tape.

The hatnip is now complete and ready to be chucked.

The tradition originated in London. Once upon a time the streets of London were so dirty and so full of rubbish that people threw things to each other across the street instead of stepping through all the mess. When someone was very hungry and had run out of bowler hats and turnips, he or she would ring a bell and open the window, hopefully. Any of the neighbours across the street who had some spare, and who wanted a bit of fun, would try to chuck a hatnip through the open window across the street.

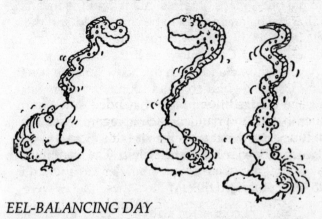

EEL-BALANCING DAY

The 30th of February is Eel-Balancing Day. This ancient custom takes place at a very secret place where certain people whose names begin with 'O' have to balance eels on the tips of their noses. However, before they can do this they have to catch their eels. Let us listen to the words of Oliver Oldham - he's now 96, but remembers going out to catch his eels as a young man:

'Oh, ar, we used ter go out before dawn, and we used ter creep through the shallow water looking out for them snoozing eels. When I saw one, I'd get me net right under 'im, tickle his tummy for a bit, then, just as 'e was 'avin' a nice dream, whip 'im out o' the water and into a big tank ...'

This tank would then be carried back to the secret place, as long as someone could remember where it was, and the carriers sang the traditional Eel-Balancer's Song on the way:

'You have to bring the eel to heel
　　And get his toes upon your nose
And balance him up with loads of zeal
　　And get to the Cow afore it close.'

The 'Cow' mentioned in the last line is not an animal but a place of refreshment, and the meaning is that the balancing has to be completed and the eels put back into the water in time for everyone to get to the Dun Cow pub for a little something. Anyone who fails to reach the 'Cow' in time has to run through a goldfish pond six times wearing a kilt and a large brown paper bag.

Eel-balancing is still carried on, according to Oliver Oldham, but the place where it is supposed to take place is now so secret that hardly anyone ever finds it.

OPEN A FOLK MUSEUM

Traditions are connected with folk-lore, and things of the countryside generally. A lot of work has been done all over the country to collect folk stories and traditions, as well as all the bits and pieces, like old ploughs and kitchen ware, that go with them. It's become big business and thousands of people visit Folk Museums every year.

But some of the bits and pieces are so small or so odd that they really could be anything. So, why not open your own Folk Museum? You'll soon find funny things to exhibit, as the idea is to give everything a really complicated label. You can put anything on show - as long as the label is convincing, who'll be able to tell the difference between your stuff and the real thing?

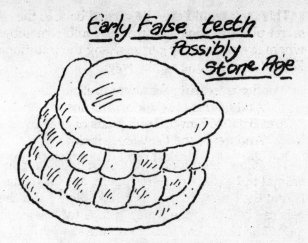

Early False teeth
possibly
Stone Age

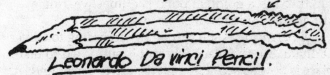

note Leonardo teeth marks

Leonardo Da Vinci Pencil.

smartie belonging
to Shirley Temple.

- note sucked white.

A carrot
that was nibbled
by Bugs Bunny.

Charge 5p admission and offer special souvenirs (like 'A Piece of Old England' for £5 - which is just a matchbox full of earth).

WELL, WELL, WELL ...

Cheer yourself up if you're ill! Cheer up a friend if he's ill! Cheer up the doctor if he's ill! Only, take care not to overdo it - he might die laughing ...

★

PATIENT: 'Will my chickenpox be better by next week?'
DOCTOR: 'I'm afraid I can't make rash promises.'

★

'Doctor, doctor, I keep seeing red and yellow flags.'
'Have you seen a psychiatrist?'
'No. Just red and yellow flags.'

★

OPTICIAN: 'You think you have bad eyesight? Well, just read the line of letters on the bottom of that card.'
PATIENT: 'What card?'

'Doctor, my family think I'm mad because I like bananas.'
'Oh, that's perfectly normal - I like bananas, too.'
'Do you? You must come round and see my collection - I've got thousands!'

'Madam, your husband must have absolute rest.'
'But doctor, he won't listen to me ...'
'Well, that's a good start.'

★

'Did you take your husband's temperature as I told you, Mrs Murphy?'
'Yes indeed, doctor, I put a barometer on his chest, and it said "very dry" so I bought him a pint of beer, and he's gone back to work.'

'Oh doctor, I'm so sorry to drag you all this way into the country on such a bad night.'
'That's all right - I have another patient near here, so I can kill two birds with one stone.'

★

The pretty girl had been examined by the doctor.
'You've got acute appendicitis,' he said at last.
'Doctor, I've come here to be examined, not admired,' said the young lady.

★

YOUNG DOCTOR: 'Why do you always ask patients what they had for their dinner?'
OLD DOCTOR: 'Well, according to their menus, I make out my bills.'

'Well, madam, what is the matter with your husband?'
'I'm afraid, doctor, he's worrying about money.'
'Ah! I think I can relieve him of that.'

FARMER PATIENT: 'And how's lawyer Smith, doctor?'
DOCTOR: 'He's lying at death's door, I'm afraid.'
FARMER: 'Yes - at death's door - and still lying.'

The medical paper asked: 'What would you do in the case of a person eating poisonous mushrooms?' The student wrote: 'Recommend a change of diet.'

DOCTOR: 'Well, Willie, how are you today?'
WILLIE: 'All right, I guess, doctor, but I'm having trouble with my breathing.'
DOCTOR: 'I must see if I can give you something to stop that.'

SOME INTERESTING ILLNESSES

strained clavichord
sponge fingers (a Victorian ailment)
fish fingers
weasels (like measles only with spots and fur)
Kentucky-fried chickenpox
pink fever (a mild form of scarlet fever)
drastic gastric flu (patient is laid low)
elastic gastric flu (patient is laid wall-to-wall)
plastic gastric flu (patient is not bio-degradable)

AND 'MUCH-BETTER, THANK-YOU' JOKES

HEDGEHOG (to his friend Freddy Frog): 'At least you're in there with a chance; whoever heard of a princess kissing a hedgehog?'

A pretty girl went into a dress shop, and asked the assistant if she could try on the dress in the window.
'I wish you would,' said the assistant, 'it would be very good for business.'

WATER BAILIFF: 'You can't fish without a permit.'
ANGLER: 'Oh, it's all right thanks, I'm doing fine with this worm.'

Paddy was marooned on a desert island. One day the tide brought in a canoe, so Paddy broke it up and made himself a raft.

BOOK SALESMAN: 'This book will do half your work for you.'
BUSINESSMAN: 'Good. I'll take two.'

'What would I get,' enquired the man who had just insured his property against fire, 'if this building should burn down tonight?'

'I would say,' replied the insurance agent, 'about ten years.'

★

TEACHER: 'Ben, why don't you wash your face? I can see what you had for breakfast this morning.'
BEN: 'What was it, Teacher?'
TEACHER: 'Egg.'
BEN: 'Wrong, Teacher. That was yesterday.'

ROBERTA: 'Will you take me for a drive on Sunday?'
ROBERT: 'Yes, but suppose it rains?'
ROBERTA: 'Well, in that case, come the day before.'

★

MARY: 'Do you allow a man to kiss you when you're out motoring with him?'
JANE: 'Certainly not. If a man can drive safely while kissing me, he's not giving the kiss the attention it deserves.'

POTTY POEMS

Potty poems, loony limericks and odd odes of every
kind are very useful to know when you want to be
funny. You can whisper these verses in the quiet bits
of horror films, or sing them in the swimming pool, or
write them in people's autograph books. They're bound
to cause a titter or two whatever you do with them!

★

There was a young lady named Rose,
Who had a huge wart on her nose.
   When she had it removed
   Her appearance improved,
But her glasses slipped down to her toes.

★

There was a strange fellow from Cork,
Who took his pet toad for a walk.
   When they asked, 'Is it tame?'
   He replied, 'Yes, its name
Is Therese and it lives upon pork.'

There was a young man from Nepal,
Who was asked to a fancy-dress ball.
   He said, 'Oh, I'll risk it
   And go as a biscuit.'
But the dog ate him up in the hall.

There was a young lady of Leeds,
Who swallowed a packet of seeds.
   In a month, silly lass,
   She was covered with grass,
And she couldn't sit down for the weeds.

There was a young man called Davy,
Who hated the food in the Navy.
   He couldn't have beef,
   In case his false teeth
Would drop out and fall in the gravy.

There was a young man of Devizes,
Whose ears were of different sizes.
   The one that was small
   Was no use at all,
But the other won several prizes.

I wish I had your picture,
   It would be very nice.
I'd hang it in the attic
   To scare away the mice.

If you build a better mousetrap,
   And put it in your house,
Before long, Mother Nature
   Will build a better mouse.

A major, with wonderful force,
Called out in Hyde Park for a horse.
   All the flowers looked round,
   But no horse could be found,
So he just rhododendron, of course.

History's a dreadful subject,
Dead as it can be.
Once it killed the Romans,
And now it's killing me.

Willie poisoned his father's tea;
    Father died in agony.
Mother came, and looked quite vexed:
    'Really, Will,' she said, 'what next?'

Into the cistern little Willie
Pushed his little sister Lily.
Mother couldn't find our daughter:
Now we sterilise our water.

A flea and a fly met in a flue,
Said the flea to the fly, 'What shall we do?'
    'Let's flee,' said the fly.
    'Let's fly,' said the flea.
And they flew through a flaw in the flue.

Here lies the body of Anna,
Done to death by a banana.
It wasn't the fruit that laid her low,
But the skin of the thing that made her go.

I eat my peas with honey,
I've done it all my life.
It makes the peas taste funny,
But it keeps them on the knife!

The Awful Adventures of Fergus on his School Trip to London

Little Fergus was a brat
The whole of London wondered at.
He dropped a stink-bomb in St Paul's
Just to see how fast it falls.
He caught a raven in the Tower,
And covered it with glue and flour -
Until Beefeaters nabbed him quick
And said, 'A raven lunatic!'
Next, Fergus in Trafalgar Square
Pea-shootered all the pigeons there,
And up old Nelson's column shinned
To wave a conker in the wind.
When Fergus sang outside the Ritz,
The windows splintered into bits.
And when he whistled in the Zoo
The beasts all started howling, too.
Next Fergus sauntered to Tussaud's
To see the waxen Queens and Lords,
But in the Horror-Chamber grim
The public all recoiled at him.
'It's time for home,' his teacher said.
'We've painted this old town quite red!
So come on children, mount the bus!'
Said Fergus, 'They'll remember US!!'

FUN WITH WORDS

Some words - like 'pong' or 'ichthyosaurus' - just
sound funny without your having to do anything
with them. However, you won't be thought very
funny if you stand and say, 'zeuglodontoid' or
'inconcinnity' - that is, if you can say them! You'll
probably just get a bucket of ice-cold water thrown
over you, so why not try the games here? Word
Riddles are like ordinary riddles. Instead of a pun,
they are letter jokes. If you have a look at them,
you'll soon understand how they work. With the
Word Quiz, you have to choose the right meaning
for the given word. This gets quite difficult, but
don't worry if you can't do them - the wrong
meanings are quite amusing, and you can make up
your own word quizzes with funny definitions as
soon as you've looked at a few of the ones here.

WORD RIDDLES

How can you spell 'chilly' with two letters?
>   *I.C.*

What letter stands for a drink?
>   *The letter T.*

What did the boy say when he opened his piggy
bank and found nothing?
>   *O.I.C.U.R.M.T.*

How can you spell 'rot' with two letters?
>   *D.K.*

What letter is like a vegetable?
>   *The letter P.*

What word grows smaller when you add two letters to it?

Add 'er' to short and it becomes shorter.

How many letters are there in the alphabet?

Eleven. T-H-E A-L-P-H-A-B-E-T.

Why is the letter B hot?

Because it makes oil boil.

What is never out of sight?

The letter S.

What is the beginning of eternity,
    The end of time and space;
The beginning of every end,
    And the end of every race?
        The letter E.

When is it correct to say, 'I is?'

'I is the letter after H.'

Why is the letter N the most powerful letter?

Because it's in the middle of TNT.

What roman numeral can climb a wall?

IV.

How do you spell 'we' with two letters without using the letters W and E?

U and I.

How do you spell 'very happy' with three letters?

X.T.C.

If you add 2-forget and 2-forget, what do you get?

4-gotten.

WORLD QUIZ

Test your word-power and make yourself laugh with this crazy word quiz. The words get more difficult as you go along.

1. What is a BUNION?
   - (a) a sort of Italian onion
   - (b) an Easter cake
   - (c) a painful lump on your foot
   - (d) a baby's toy

2. What is to THROTTLE?
   - (a) to dance energetically
   - (b) to strangle somebody
   - (c) to rinse a bottle
   - (d) to fish for squid

3. What is a FENDER?
   - (a) the surround to a fireplace
   - (b) someone who saves penalties
   - (c) a sort of cucumber
   - (d) a defence lawyer

4. What is SHINGLE?
   (a) a food like porridge
   (b) a rock group
   (c) a game played in Ireland
   (d) pebbles on the beach

5. What is PREDICTION?
   (a) something long and slimy in the undergrowth
   (b) a strong drink
   (c) a special way of speaking
   (d) a forecast for the future

6. What is GORGONZOLA?
   (a) a mad monster living in a Greek cave
   (b) a sort of Italian cheese
   (c) a French novelist living on the dole
   (d) the name of one of the Queen's corgis

7. What is a MANDOLIN?
   (a) a strange stringed instrument
   (b) a little orange from Seville
   (c) a strange little monkey
   (d) a plaster

8. What is CORNUCOPIA?
   (a) a photocopying machine
   (b) a cure for hard skin on the feet
   (c) a horn of plenty
   (d) a man with a horse's legs

9. What is HYPOCHONDRIA?
   (a) fear of dogs
   (b) a Roman central-heating system
   (c) fear of central heating
   (d) thinking you're ill when you're not

10. What is a SQUINT?
    (a) a baby octopus
    (b) a firework
    (c) an irregularity of the eyes
    (d) an Ethiopian coin

11. What is CROQUET?
    (a) a kind of knitting
    (b) a potato rissole
    (c) a tall hat
    (d) a ball and hoop game

12. What is a QUADRUPED?
    (a) a college playground
    (b) something folded four times
    (c) an animal with four legs
    (d) a mountain pass

13. What is a GROTTO?
    (a) the part of a town occupied by racial minorities
    (b) an underground cavern
    (c) an italian dish
    (d) a musical instrument

14. What is a QUAIL?
    (a) a feathered pen
    (b) a shiver down your spine
    (c) a bird
    (d) a quantity of paper

15. What is a VIPER?
    (a) a cleaning cloth
    (b) a poisonous snake
    (c) a stage whisper
    (d) part of a lady's underclothes

16. What is a VALISE?
    (a) a gentleman's servant
    (b) a regiment of the Guards
    (c) a mattress made of straw
    (d) a suitcase

17. What is PLATINUM?
    (a) a fountain pen
    (b) the largest possible number of something
    (c) a metal
    (d) a web-footed animal

18. What is a TUMBRIL?
    (a) a machine used for drying laundry
    (b) a wagon used in the French Revolution
    (c) the icy wastes of the Frozen North
    (d) an acrobat

19. What is an ANAGRAM?
 (a) a great-grandmother
 (b) an old-fashioned record-player
 (c) a district between France and Spain
 (d) letters in a word rearranged to make
      another word

20. What is a RESOLUTION?
 (a) an uprising
 (b) a recollection
 (c) determination
 (d) the agenda of a meeting

21. What is a GOURMAND?
 (a) a greedy eater
 (b) a plant similar to a cucumber
 (c) a pigsty
 (d) a type of goldfish

22. What is an EGRESS?
    (a) a baby eagle
    (b) a species of heron
    (c) a black lady
    (d) an outlet or exit

23. What is a BUSTARD?
    (a) a yellow sauce
    (b) a hot condiment
    (c) a bird similar to an ostrich
    (d) a jerkin made of buckskin

24. What is ORATORY?
    (a) a church collection
    (b) a figurative manner of speaking or writing
    (c) an eloquent speech
    (d) a sandy patch of earth

25. What is a COCOON?
    (a) a subdivision of a regiment
    (b) a ribbon stuck in a hat like a badge
    (c) a covering spun by certain insects for
        protection
    (d) a bird which nests in the nests of other
        birds.

ANSWERS TO WORD QUIZ

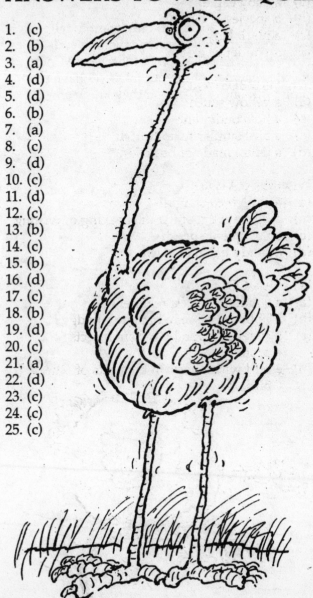

1. (c)
2. (b)
3. (a)
4. (d)
5. (d)
6. (b)
7. (a)
8. (c)
9. (d)
10. (c)
11. (d)
12. (c)
13. (b)
14. (c)
15. (b)
16. (d)
17. (c)
18. (b)
19. (d)
20. (c)
21. (a)
22. (d)
23. (c)
24. (c)
25. (c)

DASH · DOT · DOT · DASH ·

Some jokes are so good you only want to tell them
to a few select friends - so write them in code. If
you give your friends a copy of the Morse Code
below they can decipher your joke and have fun
sending back one of theirs - if they know any!

A	· —
B	— · · ·
C	— · — ·
D	— · ·
E	·
F	· · — ·
G	— — ·
H	· · · ·
I	· ·
J	· — — —
K	— · —
L	· — · ·
M	— —
N	— ·
O	— — —
P	· — — ·
Q	— — · —
R	· — ·
S	· · ·
T	—
U	· · —
V	· · · —
W	· — —
X	— · · —
Y	— · — —
Z	— — · ·

Figures:

1	· — — — —	6	— · · · ·
2	· · — — —	7	— — · · ·
3	· · · — —	8	— — — · ·
4	· · · · —	9	— — — — ·
5	· · · · ·	10	— — — — —

See if you can decipher this quip:

— · — · / · — / — · / — · / — · · / · — · · / · / · · · / /
— — / · — / — · — / · / / · — · · / · · / — — · /
· · · · / — / / — — / · / · · — / · — · / · · · / /

Remember that one stroke means a new letter, and two strokes mean a new word.

You can invent your own codes. You could try using numbers for letters, for example:

A = 5	F = 12	K = 4
B = 8	G = 2	L = 19
C - 24	H = 7	M = 21
D = 18	I = 3	N = 26
E = 13	J = 10	

and so on. You needn't just use the numbers 1–26; any range can be used. Make sure you have a name for each of the codes so that when you send a joke to someone you can indicate which code it's in. Then your friend will get the joke, and not a piece of nonsense.

Incidentally …

FRED: 'What sort of illness does a Secret Agent have all the time?'
TED: 'A code in the nose!'

YULE LAUGH AT THIS

Christmas is a great time for traditional fun. After Christmas dinner everyone probably falls asleep, having eaten too much of everything; but when the family has had a doze, get Christmas Day going again with an imaginative game of:

CHARADES

You have to choose an action - such as pulling in a ship's anchor, or being a taxi-driver and picking up a passenger - and act it out as well as you can. When you've done your bit, and everyone's crying, 'Brilliant!' or 'Get off!', you must demand to know from them what it was you were doing. Whoever guesses has to act out the next charade.

If everyone's just too tired to move, you can describe what you would have done had you not had that fourth helping of pudding. These charades can be much more complicated, and to get you going, here are some examples:

CHARADE NO. 1

'I'm crouched on the table and curled up into a ball. There's steam rising from my body, and custard running down my neck from the large dollop on my head. What am I?'
WHAT THEY'LL SAY:
    'You're a Christmas Pudding!'
YOUR ANSWER:
    'No. I'm Mount Etna after an eruption!'

CHARADE NO. 2

Stretch out flat on the table. Get your little sister to pull your feet and your big brother to pull your hands. Then you go BANG! and they both fall backwards.

WHAT THEY'LL SAY:

'You're a cracker!'

YOUR ANSWER:

'It's very nice of you to say so, but we were enacting the splitting of the atom.'

CAROL CHARADES

Another sort of charade is where you act out the title of a carol, e.g. 'The Boar's Head'.

When Uncle Pete is droning on: 'We thought we'd take the A6097 to Much Crashing but we missed the turn and found ourselves on the Great Snoring bypass and so we had to take the B7432 to Milton Windwiper and that put an extra 20 minutes on ...'

Place Uncle Pete's head on a serving-dish (you can detach it from his body if you really want to cheer the family up!). And there you have it: 'The Bore's Head'!

Or you can try 'Ding Dong Merrily on High'.

Send your sister and her boyfriend up onto the landing and as they leave the room, whisper to your sister, 'I saw him with Rita Tweeter the other night.' Soon, they'll be having a fine old row up there.

'You told me you had an Evening Class on Thursdays.'

'Well, I do.'

'What's all this about Rita, then? You pig!'

'There's no need to fly off the handle. You're so jealous!'

And here, to the listening family downstairs, it's clear: there's a 'Ding Dong Merrily on High'.

ANIMAL MAGIC

Animals really know how to be funny without trying. Penguins waddle, monkeys leap about and the sea-lions make funny honking noises.

Here are some games for any time you want to be as funny as the funniest animals you know.

IMITATIONS

Straight imitations of animals make a good party game, and if you develop your own skills you can amuse your friends any time with your impressions of the zoo!

MIME

Try showing how an animal would do an everyday thing. You don't make a single noise. Get your friends to guess what the animal is, and when they do, get them to do a mime. Here are a few suggestions to get things going:

A pig cooking an omelette.
A frog sweeping the floor.

A horse going shopping in a supermarket.
A chicken at a disco.

A monkey playing tennis.
A snake watching TV.
A crocodile working in the garden.

A cat posting a letter.
A dog playing the cello.
A goldfish doing a crossword puzzle.

A budgie cleaning windows.

IMITATING ANIMALS WITH NOISES ONLY

This is easier than mime, and it can cause more hilarious havoc - so don't go mad and start imitating elephants trumpeting if you're in the library! If you've got a tape-recorder, record some of your animal imitations and see if your friends can recognise them. If you haven't got one, stand behind the door so they can't see you. (They'll probably find this much more enjoyable!)

Once you've mastered the art of animal imitations, you can act out short charades based on stories, plays or songs in which animals have leading roles. Your friends have got to try to guess the title from your two-minute version. (Use animal noises and mime only, to make it more difficult!)

Some simple ones:
Dick Whittington
The Muppets
Mother Goose
The Teddy-Bears' Picnic
The Wind in the Willows
Alice in Wonderland
Noah's Flood

Then, try acting two-minute charades of well-known proverbs or sayings involving animals.
Some examples:

A bird in the hand is worth two in the bush.
Let sleeping dogs lie.
You can take a horse to water but you can't make it drink.
Don't look a gift horse in the mouth.
When the cat's away the mice will play.
A bear with a sore head.
A cat may look at a queen.

OLD JOKES ABOUT ANIMALS

There are lots of good old jokes about animals, and some pretty funny new ones, too. Learn a few of them off by heart and try them out next time you go to the zoo. Or don't wait that long, try them out on your family. They're animals, too, you know!

What's black and white with red spots?
> *A zebra with measles.*

On which side does a chicken have the most feathers?
> *On the outside.*

When is a black dog not a black dog?
> *When he's a greyhound.*

What is a parrot?
> *A wordy birdie.*

What is a calf after it is six months old?
> *Seven months old.*

What did the mother worm say to her baby when he was late for breakfast?
> *'Where in earth have you been?'*

What keys are furry?
> *Donkeys.*

Did you hear about the man who thought that the Rover 3500 was a bionic dog?

ANIMAL POEMS

Learn these rhymes and cheer everyone's flagging
spirits as they look at yet another kind of ant in the
Insect House!

Ooey Gooey was a worm,
     And a fine young worm was he.
He ventured on the railway track
     The train he did not see.
EEk! Ouch! Splatter, splutter!
Ooey Gooey's peanut butter.

I raised such a hullaballoo,
When I found a big mouse in my stew;
     Said the waiter, 'Don't shout
     And wave it about,
Or the rest will be wanting one, too!'

A wonderful bird is the sea gull.
It can fly quite as high as an eagle.
     It will sit on the sand,
     And eat from your hand,
But you can't tell a he from a she gull.

A furry old bear at the Zoo
Could always find something to do.
     When it bored him to go
     On a walk to and fro,
He went backwards and walked fro and to.

A centipede named Marguerite
Bought shoes for each one of her feet.
     'For,' she said, 'I might chance
     To go to a dance,
And I must have my outfit complete.'

A mouse in the night woke Miss Dowd,
She was frightened and screamed very loud.
    Then she thought: 'At the least
    I shall scare off the beast.'
And she sat up in bed and meowed.

Hickory, dickory, dock:
The mice ran up the clock!
The clock struck one -
The rest escape with minor injuries.

FAVOURITES

Mother: Jonathan's taking ten 'O' levels this summer.
Friend: Is he going to have a coach?
Mother: No, it'll only be a new bike if he gets them.

Patient: Doctor, I've got back trouble.
Doctor: You're telling me! You're back every five minutes.

A patient said to his doctor, 'Doctor, my arms hurt me, my stomach hurts me, my chest hurts me, my neck and shoulders hurt, and my head hurts too.'

'Just relax while I examine you,' said the doctor. He picked up a small hammer and tapped the patient's knee to test his reflexes. 'How do you feel now?' he enquired.

'Now my knee hurts too!' groaned the patient.

Policeman: Madam, do you know what gear you were in when you had the car accident?
Woman: Yes, officer, I was wearing a pink blouse, black skirt and white shoes.

Man: (on underground train): Excuse me, miss, would you like to share my strap?

Girl: No thank you, I already have one.

Man: No, you haven't, that's my tie you're hanging on to.

'Have I shown you my holiday photos?'
'No, and I appreciate it.'

Two elephants were courting and decided to get married.
'And who knows,' whispered one to the other, 'one day we may hear the thunder of little feet.'

Hiawatha: We don't seem to get any smoke signals from Sitting Bull these days.

Minnehaha: No, he's given up his old fire and got central heating instead.

Mrs. Gargoyle: Why is your husband jumping up and down like that?

Mrs. Cookson: Because the doctor told him to take four pills a day, then skip a day.

Waiter: What would you like to drink, sir?
Customer: I'll have some ginger beer.
Waiter: Pale?
Customer: Oh no, a glass will do.

Question: Five people stood under one umbrella. Why didn't they get wet?
Answer: It wasn't raining.

A policeman saw an old man pulling a box on a lead down a busy street.

'Poor man,' he thought, 'I'd better humour him.'

He went up to the old man and said:

'That's a nice dog you've got there.'

'It isn't a dog, it's a box,' replied the old man.

'Oh, I'm sorry,' said the policeman, 'I thought you were a bit simple,' and he walked on.

The old man looked at the box and said:

'We fooled him that time, didn't we Rover?'

Did you hear about the cat who joined the Red Cross?

He wanted to be a first aid kit.

Susan: That boy over there's annoying me.
Anne: He's not even looking at you.
Susan: I know, that's what's annoying me.

'My dog is so lazy you have to wag his tail for him.'
'Well, mine's so slow that he usually fetches yesterday's paper.'

Girl: Do you believe in love at first sight?
Vampire: No, I believe in love at first bite.

Tom: You know Lake Windermere? Well, my dad dug the hole for it.

Tim: You know the Dead Sea? Well, my dad killed it.

Teacher: What is your name?

New boy: Francis Mickey Brown.

Teacher: In that case, I shall call you Francis Brown.

New boy: My dad won't like that.

Teacher: Why not?

New boy: He doesn't like anyone taking the Mickey out of my name.

John: How's your sister getting on with her diet?

Dave: Great! She disappeared last week.

While decorating a house a man fell from the top of a ladder. Later he told his wife that four ribs were broken.

'Four ribs broken!' she exclaimed, 'Which hospital did you go to?'

'I didn't have to go to hospital.'

'Four ribs broken and you didn't have to go to hospital?'

'No, it was the bloke I landed on whose ribs were broken.'

Waiter: After the steak I recommend a trifle.
Customer: Judging by the size of the steak, I think I've already had it.

Psychiatrist: I understand your husband thinks that he is a car.
Mrs. Morris: That's right, doctor.
Psychiatrist: You must bring him in straight away.
Mrs. Morris: I can't, he's double parked outside.

'My grandad is famous. He invented glue.'
'I bet he's stuck up.'

Simple Simon: Do you have breakfast in the morning?
Smart Alec: Of course, stupid. If I had it at noon it would be lunch.

Patient: Tell it to me straight, doctor, how long have I got left to live?
Doctor: Well! I wouldn't buy any long playing records if I were you.

An old lady was on her way home one very dark night. On turning a corner she bumped into an old man and they both fell flat on the ground. The old man was very apologetic.

'That's alright,' said the old lady, 'I'm not hurt, but would you be so kind as to point me in the direction I was going before you knocked me down.'

Doctor:	And how are those Strength Pills that I gave you working, Mr. Weakling.
Mr. Weakling:	They're not.
Doctor:	You mean they're not having any effect at all?
Mr. Weakling:	No, I can't get the lid off the bottle.

Did you hear about the man who was so mean that on Christmas Eve he went outside and fired a gun, and then came back and told his children that Father Christmas had committed suicide.

How do fishermen make nets?
They just sew a lot of holes together.

The teacher noticed that Frank had been staring out of the window for some time, so she decided to catch his attention.

'Frank,' she said, 'if the world is 25,000 miles round and eggs are 62p. a dozen, how old am I?'

'Thirty-two,' said Frank.

The teacher blushed and asked:

'How did you know that?'

'It was easy,' said Frank. 'My sister is sixteen and she's only half mad.

Doctor: Why did you jump in that river to retrieve your hat? You could have been killed.

Patient: I know, but I had to get my hat back, doctor. If I go without one in the winter, I catch cold.

Judge: William Toomey, you were arrested for stealing an elephant. Why did you steal an elephant?

William: Because my dad said: 'Willie, if your gonna steal, steal big'.

Teacher: Right, Lou Ellen, how much is 5 and 5?

Lou Ellen: Nine.

Teacher: No, it's not. It's ten.

Lou Ellen: It can't be ten. Yesterday you told me 6 and 4 were ten.

Why is Tibet the noisiest country in the world? Because everywhere you go it's yak, yak, yak.

'I got fired from my job as a waiter because I'm too tough. I don't take orders from anybody.'

A policeman was walking along Primrose Lane when he saw a man on his hands and knees on the pavement.

'Can I help you, sir?' asked the policeman.

'Oh, it's alright officer. It's just that I dropped my watch in Chignall Road.'

'Then why are you looking for it in Primrose Lane if you dropped it in Chignall Road?'

'Because there's more light here.'

What noise does a horse make going backwards? Cloppity clip, cloppity clip.

An American visiting Australia was asked by the Australian host:

'Do you like our bridge here at Sydney Harbour?'

'Oh, we've got bridges much bigger than that,' said the American.

'And what do you think of our marvellous Opera House?' asked the Australian.

'We've got buildings twice the size of that,' exclaimed the American.

Just then a kangaroo went bounding by. 'Well,' said the American. 'I've got to admit one thing. Your grasshoppers are a little larger than ours.'

How can you tell when someone has a glass eye? If it comes out in conversation.

Old Lady: These mothballs you sold me last week are no good.

Shopkeeper: Why's that.

Old Lady: I haven't hit a single moth with them.

A fat man in a cinema turned to the seat behind him.

'Can you see, little boy?'

'No, I can't!' said the boy.

'Well,' said the fat man, 'just watch me and laugh when I do.'

A young nurse was watching an operation for the first time.

'What are you doing?' she asked the surgeon.

'This man swallowed a golf ball,' he told her, 'and we're trying to remove it from his throat.'

'And I suppose the worried looking man outside is the patient's father,' said the nurse.

'No,' said the surgeon, 'it's his partner and he's waiting to get on with the game.'

What did Simple Simon say when he had finished
cutting the lawn with nail scissors?
'That's all there is, there isn't any mower.'

Guest: Didn't you say that this boarding house
was only a stone's throw from the sea?
Landlady: Yes, keep practising. You'll soon be able
to throw it two miles.

What jewels do ghosts wear?
Tomb stones.

I live in a tough neighbourhood. On Christmas Eve
I hung my stockings up over the fireplace and
Father Christmas stole them.

A woman patient in the dentist's chair opened her
mouth as wide as she could.
    'You don't have to open that wide,' said the
dentist, 'I don't plan to stand inside.'

'It was so cold last week, my grandma's teeth were
chattering, and they weren't even in her mouth.'

1st Nurse: Let me see, how many patients has
that new doctor had. I think it's three.
2nd Nurse: No, I'm positive it's four. I'm sure
because I attended all four funerals.

A man rang the hospital to see how his wife was
and whether she had given birth to her baby yet.
    'Is this her first child?' asked the nurse.
    'No, this is her husband.'

Man: Do you let your dog lie on the couch?
Friend: Only when he visits the psychiatrist.

Simon: Did your dad promise you something if you cut the grass?
Nigel: No, but he promised me something if I didn't.

Teacher: Do you know the capital of Alaska?
Martha: Juneau?
Teacher: Of course I know, but I'm asking you.

A man walked into a shop selling fabrics and said:
  'I'd like three yards of satan for my wife.'
  'You mean satin, sir,' said the assistant. 'Satan is something that looks like the devil.'
  'Oh, you've seen my wife then!'

ELEPHANTS TO FORGET

What's the difference between an elephant and a bison?
You can't wash your hands in an elephant.

What did the hotel manager say to the elephant who wouldn't pay his bill?
'Pack your trunk and get out!'

Why are elephants grey and wrinkled?
Have you ever tried ironing an elephant?

How can you tell if there's an elephant sleeping in your bed?
Look for the peanut shells between the sheets.

Jack: What's the difference between an elephant and a matterbaby?
Jill: What's a matterbaby?
Jack: Nothing, what's wrong with you?

What time is it when an elephant sits on your fence?
Time to get a new fence.

Hickory, dickory dock,
The elephant ran up the clock.
The clock is being repaired.

Why do elephants wear green felt hats?
So that they can walk across billiard tables without
being seen.

What is big, grey and mutters?
A mumbo jumbo.

How do you get four elephants into a car?
Two in the front and two in the back.

How do you get four giraffes into the same car?
Wait until the elephants get out.

When do elephants have sixteen feet?
When there are four of them.

What does an elephant do when it rains?
Gets wet.

How can you tell if an elephant has been in your
refrigerator?
Look for footprints in the butter.

How can you tell if an elephant is under your bed?
When your head hits the ceiling.

Why did the elephant wear ripple-soled shoes?
To give the ants a 50-50 chance.

A woman sat on a bus eating peanuts. Trying to be friendly, she offered some to the woman sitting beside her.

'Goodness, no!' said the woman, 'Peanuts are so fattening.'

'What makes you think that?' asked the first woman.

'My dear, have you ever seen a slim elephant?'

Why does an elephant wear plimsolls?
To sneak up on mice.

Alfie elephant: How was your trip to America?
Ena elephant: Okay, apart from my day in Alabama.
Alfie elephant: What was wrong with that?
Ena elephant: There's a city called Tusk-a-loosa. I'd only been there two hours when one of my tusks fell off.

What would happen if you crossed an elephant with a kangaroo?
You'd get great big holes all over Australia.

Why are elephants found in Africa?
Because they're so big, they don't get lost.

How do you tell when you're in bed with an elephant?
By the big 'E' on his pyjama jacket.

Mick: How can you tell an elephant from a banana?
Dick: Try and pick it up. If you can't it's an elephant.

Why did the elephant paint himself all different colours?
So he could hide in a crayon box.

How do you tell an elephant from a monster?
A monster never remembers.

How can you tell if an elephant has been in your bedroom?
By the wrinkled sheets and the strong smell of peanuts.

What is the difference between a flea and an elephant?
An elephant can have fleas, but a flea can't have elephants.

What is worse than a giraffe with a shore throat?
An elephant with a nosebleed.

What's grey, has four legs and a trunk?
A mouse going on holiday.

Inquirer: I want to put an advertisement in your paper.
Telephonist: Is it to go in the small ads, sir?
Inquirer: Oh, no. I want to sell an elephant.

Why do elephants wear sandals?
To stop themselves sinking in the sand.

Why do ostriches bury their heads in the sand?
To look for elephants who aren't wearing sandals.

Why is an elephant large, grey and wrinkled?
Because if he was small, round and white he'd be
an aspirin.

How much did the psychiatrist charge the
elephant?
£15 for the visit and £150 for the couch.

What should you do when an elephant breaks a
toe?
Ring for a tow truck.

Did you hear about the elephant that went to the
seaside to see something new in trunks?

What do you call an elephant that flies?
A Jumbo jet.

Which is stronger, a snail or an elephant?
A snail because it carries its house. An elephant
only carries its trunk.

What is yellow outside, grey inside, and has a
wonderful memory?
An elephant omelette.

Where can you buy ancient elephants?
At a mammoth sale.

How do you catch an elephant?
Make a noise like a peanut.

What is red outside, grey inside, and very
crowded?
A bus full of elephants.

Why don't elephants ride bicycles?
Because their thumbs can't ring the bells.

What goes clomp, clomp, clomp, swish?
An elephant with wet plimsolls.

What is big and green and has a trunk?
An unripe elephant.

Why don't elephants like penguins?
Because they can't get the paper off.

Why are elephants grey?
So you won't mistake them for strawberries.

What does an elephant have that no other animal
has?
A baby elephant.

What do you do when an elephant has a cold?
Run like mad if he sneezes.

What do you get if you cross an elephant with a mouse?
Great big holes in your skirting board.

Two elephants fell off a cliff.
Boom! Boom!

Why do elephants paint the soles of their feet yellow?
So that they can float upside down in custard.

What did the elephant rock star say over the microphone?
Tusking, tusking, one, two, three, four ...

'Do you allow elephants on this train?'
'Yes, but we have to check their trunks.'

What did Tarzan say when he saw the elephants come towards him?
'Here come the elephants.'

What did Tarzan say when he saw the elephants coming with sunglasses on?
Nothing. He didn't recognise them.

Why do elephants drink so much water?
Nobody offers them anything else.

What did the grape say when the elephant trod on it?
Nothing. It just let out a little wine.

Why do elephants paint their toenails red?
So that they can hide in cherry trees.

Tom: Have you ever seen an elephant in a cherry tree?
Dick: No.
Tom: See how well it works then.

How would an elephant smell without his trunk?
He'd still smell awful!

What's the difference between an elephant and an apple?
Have you ever tried peeling an elephant?

What do you have to know to teach an elephant tricks?
More than the elephant.

Elephant trainer: Doctor, my elephant has just swallowed a bullet, what shall I do?
Doctor: Just don't point his trunk at anyone.

'I can lift an elephant with one hand.'
'But where can you find a one-handed elephant?'

Sybil: Do you really play chess with your elephant? He must be very clever.
Cyril: Not really. I beat him most of the time.

A small girl was telling a friend about her visit to the zoo.
'And I saw the elephants,' she explained, 'and you'll never guess what they were doing.'
'I don't know, what were they doing?' asked her friend.
'They were picking up peanuts with their vacuum cleaners.'

What's the difference between an African elephant and an Indian elephant?
About 3,000 miles.

Why couldn't the elephants go swimming together?
Because they only had one pair of trunks between
them.

How can you tell if there's an elephant in your
oven?
You can't shut the door.

What would you do with a blue elephant?
Take him to the cinema to cheer him up.

Patient: Doctor, doctor, I keep seeing elephants
with big yellow spots.
Doctor: Have you ever seen a psychiatrist?
Patient: No, just elephants with big yellow
spots ...

What is big, grey and dangerous?
An elephant with a machine gun.

What is worse than a turtle with claustrophobia?
An elephant with a blocked nose.

Why did the elephants leave the circus?
They were tired of working for peanuts.

What do you call an elephant with earmuffs?
Anything you like; he can't hear you.

What do you do with old footballs?
Give them to elephants to play marbles.

What do you give an elephant with big feet?
Plenty of room!

'What's the difference between an elephant and a pint of milk?'
'I don't know.'
'Well, I'm certainly not sending you out for a pint of milk.'

Why do elephants wear dark glasses?
If you had all these jokes told about you, you wouldn't want to be recognised either.

MORE SIGN LANGUAGE

Sign outside hairdressers:

We Curl up and Dye for you

Sign in front of house:

Anyone is welcome to borrow our
Lawnmower as long as they don't
take it out of the garden.

Sign in King Arthur's Court:

Sign in classroom:

LAUGH AND THE CLASS LAUGHS WITH YOU,
BUT YOU STAY AFTER SCHOOL ALONE

Sign outside a petshop selling tropical fish:

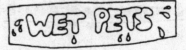

Sign on a delivery van:

Sign in cafeteria in Holland:

Mothers, Please wash your Hans
before eating.

Sign in restaurant:

Our cutlery is not medicine, and should not be taken after meals.

Sign outside travel agency:

Sign in police station:

....//////THIRTY DAYS HATH SEPTEMBER,
....////APRIL, JUNE, AND THE SPEED OFFENDER

Sign outside dress shop:

Don't stand outside and faint
—Come inside and have a fit.

Sign in street:

**AVOID THAT RUN-DOWN FEELING —
LOOK BOTH WAYS BEFORE YOU CROSS**

Sign at public speaking class:

NO SILENCE ALLOWED.

Sign outside a dry cleaners:

IF YOUR CLOTHES AREN'T BECOMING TO YOU,
THEY SHOULD BE COMING TO US.

Sign at butcher's shop:

H⊙NEST SCALES
NO TWO WEIGHS ABOUT IT.

Sign on dustcart:

SATISFACTION GUARANTEED
- or double your rubbish back

Sign in doctor's surgery:

An Apple A Day Is Bad For Business

Sign at another butcher's shop:

Pleased to meet you – Meat to please you.

Sign in funeral parlour:

SATISFACTION GUARANTEED
- or Your Mummy Back

Sign at flying school:

Sign in pet shop:

Sign in theatre:

Shakespeare married an Avon Lady

Sign in tyre shop:

WE SKID YOU NOT

Sign in hen house:

THERE'S NOTHING DISGRACEFUL
IN BEING CHICKEN

Sign in cemetery:

People are prohibited from picking flowers from any grave other than their own

Sign in garage:

DO NOT SMOKE!
If Your Life Isn't Worth Anything, Petrol Is!

Sign in department store:

Bargain Basement Upstairs

Sign on electricity pylon:

TOUCHING THESE WIRES WILL RESULT IN INSTANT DEATH.
ANYONE FOUND DOING SO WILL BE PROSECUTED.

POTTY
POEMS

Humpty Dumpty sat on a wall,
Humpty Dumpty had a great fall,
All the King's horses and all the King's men,
Had scrambled eggs for breakfast again.

There was a young girl from Japan,
Whose poetry never would scan,
   When they said it was so,
   She replied, 'Yes, I know,
But I always make it a rule to try and get just as many
words into the last line as I possibly can.'

The baker's wife, Alberta Smythe,
Had loads and loads of fun.
For every time she did her hair,
She put it in a bun.

I had written to Auntie Maud,
Who was on a trip abroad,
When I heard she'd died of cramp -
Just too late to save the stamp.

Mary had a little lamb,
You've heard this tale before,
But did you know she passed the plate,
And had a little more?

Mary had a little lamb,
A lobster and some prunes,
A glass of pop, a piece of pie,
A whole plate of macaroons.
She also ate two large cream cakes,
A portion of cod's roe;
And when they carried Mary out,
Her face was white as snow.

Little Miss Muffet sat on a tuffet,
  eating her curds and whey,
Along came a spider
  who sat down beside her
And said: 'Too much cholesterol, I'd say.'

There was an old man in a trunk,
Who inquired of his wife, 'Am I drunk?'
  She replied, with regret,
  'I'm afraid so, my pet,'
And he answered, 'That's just as I thunk.'

The bottle of perfume that Willie sent
Was highly displeasing to Millicent.
  Her thanks were so cold,
  They quarrelled, I'm told,
Through that silly scent Willie sent Millicent.

There was a young lady of Diss
Who thought skating was absolute bliss.
  Till love turned to hate
  When a slip of her skate

Made her finish up something like this.

Jimmy Rose
Sat on a pin
Jimmy rose.

Don't worry if your life's a joke,
And your successes few,
Remember that the mighty oak,
Was once a nut like you.

I SAY! I SAY! I SAY!

Why is your nose in the middle of your face?
Because it is the scenter.

What do you get if you dial 0178964572309862349?
A sore finger.

What should you do if you find a gorilla sleeping in
your bed?
Sleep somewhere else.

What did one tap say to the other?
You're a big drip.

Who always tries to make you smile?
A photographer.

Did the cock fall in love with the hen at first sight?
No, she egged him on a bit.

Why are dentists artistic?
Because they are good at drawing teeth.

Why are waiters willing to learn?
Because they are always prepared to take tips from people.

Where are whales weighed?
At a whale weigh station.

What sort of tiles can't be stuck on a wall?
Reptiles.

What did the bus conductor say to the one-legged man?
Hop on.

Who is the smallest mother in the world?
Minimum.

There were two bishops in a bed. Which one wore the nightie?
Mrs. Bishop.

How can you write a composition with just two letters?
Write an SA.

What do people always cry over?
Onions.

What animal can you never trust?
A cheetah.

When is your mind like a rumpled bed?
When it isn't made up.

What do Eskimos call their cows?
Eskimoos.

What do you say to a monster with three heads?
Hello, hello, hello.

What are the last three hairs of a dog's tail called?
Dog's hairs.

What do you get if you cross a mink with a kangaroo?
A fur coat with pockets.

Where did Noah keep his bees?
In ark hives.

Why was Adam known as a good runner?
Because he was first in the human race.

If Ireland should sink, which city would float?
Cork.

The more there is of it, the less you see of it. What is it?
Darkness.

What do you get if you are hit on the head with an axe?
A splitting headache.

If an egg floated down the River Thames, where would it have come from?
A chicken.

How can you double your money?
Fold it in half.

What do punks learn in school?
Punctuation.

What is the chiropodist's theme song?
There's no business like toe business.

What is French for idiot?
Lagoon.

What ring is square?
A boxing ring.

Which nuts grow on walls?
Walnuts.

What goes 'Ho, ho, ho, plop'?
Santa Claus laughing his head off.

What is a crick?
The noise of a Japanese camera.

What did the ceiling say to the chandelier?
'You're the only bright spot in my life.'

Why are doctors like boxers?
They're always jabbing people.

What happens to illegally parked frogs?
They get toad away.

What do you get if you cross an elephant with a
boy scout?
An elephant that helps old ladies across the road.

Where do mummies swim?
In the Dead Sea.

Why did the chicken run away from home?
It was tired of being cooped up.

What do you get if you cross a chicken with a guitar?
A chicken that makes music when you pluck it.

What kind of mistake does a ghost make?
A boo-boo.

What did the policeman say to the naughty frog?
Go on, hop it.

What did Lady Hamilton say to Nelson?
You're the one-eye care for.

What do you get if you cross a policeman with a telegram?
Copper wire.

What kind of cat swims under water?
An octopus.

When is an envelope like a snooty person?
When it is stuck up.

Why don't you get custard in China?
Would you like to eat custard with chopsticks?

What made the bed spread?
It saw the pillow slip.

What is white, has just one horn, and gives milk?
A milk truck.

What is an elephant after he is four days old?
Five days old.

How did the boy feel after being caned?
Absolutely whacked.

What do call a silly monkey?
A chumpanzee.

What is at the end of everything?
The letter G.

Why is it against the law to whisper?
Because it isn't aloud.

What do you call a ghost doctor?
A surgical spirit.

What smells most in a perfumery?
Your nose.

What do you call smoke coming out of a church?
Holy smoke.

Who always has to sleep with his shoes on?
A horse.

What happened when the cat swallowed a penny?
There was some money in the kitty.

Why did the doctor give up his practice?
He kept losing his patients.

Why was Shakespeare able to write so well?
Because where there's a Will there's a way.

Which 7-letter name has only 3 letters?
Barbara.

Why does lightning shock people?
Because it doesn't know how to conduct itself.

How many letters are there in the alphabet?
Eleven: T-H-E-A-L-P-H-A-B-E-T!

What is bought by the yard and worn by the foot?
A carpet.

What happened to the man who bought a paper
shop?
It blew away.

What is musical and handy in a supermarket?
A Chopin Liszt.

What is a baby bee?
A little humbug.

What did the stag say to his children?
'Hurry up, deers.'

How can you always find a liar out?
Go to his house when he isn't in.

What will always stay hot in the refrigerator?
Mustard.

Why did the cashier steal money from the till?
She thought the change would do her good.

What is the best way to make a pair of trousers last?
Make the jacket first.

Why isn't it safe to sleep on a train?
Because trains run over sleepers.

How do sailors get their clothes clean?
They throw them overboard and they get washed ashore.

What would you call two bananas?
A pair of slippers.

Why did the chicken cross the road twice?
Because she was a double crosser.

What happened when the wheel was invented?
It caused a revolution.

Why is a piano like an eye?
Because they are both closed with their lids down.

What happens to a flea when it gets really angry?
It becomes hopping mad.

What did the Eskimo say when he finished
building his igloo?
Ours is an ice house, ours is.

Who has huge antlers and wears white gloves?
Mickey Moose.

How do you find where a flea has bitten you?
Start from scratch.

What is green, hairy and takes aspirin?
A gooseberry with a headache.

What jumps from cake to cake and tastes of
almonds?
Tarzipan.

What gives milk and says 'ooM, ooM'?

How do you make gold soup?
You start with fourteen carrots.

What kind of pine has the sharpest needles?
A porcupine.

Why should birds in a nest always agree?
Otherwise they might fall out.

What's old, grey and travels at 100 mph?
An E-type grannie.

What falls in the winter, but never gets hurt?
Snow.

What does Her Majesty the Queen do when she
burps?
She issues a Royal Pardon.

Who always succeeds?
A toothless budgie.

Why is a lord like a book?
Because they both have a title.

What is the cheapest way to hire a car?
Put bricks under the wheels.

What two letters spell jealousy?
N.V.

What is the difference between a gossip and an
umbrella?
You can shut up an umbrella.

Why are ghosts very simple things?
Because you can easily see through them.

What is a dogma?
A mother of pups.

What did Cinderella say when her photographs
didn't arrive?
Some day my prints will come.

How many beans can you put in an empty bag?
One. After that it isn't empty.

What did the musician spend all his time in bed
for?
He wrote sheet music.

What did the mouse say when it broke a tooth?
Hard cheese.

Why did the boy swallow 50p?
It was his dinner money.

What is yellow with greasy wings?
A bread and butterfly.

What happened when the sick man opened the
window?
Influenza.

Why did Adam bite the apple?
Because he hadn't got a knife.

Why is a baby worth its weight in gold?
Because it's a dear little thing.

What goes out black and comes in white?
A black dog on a snowy day.

What runs around Paris in a plastic bag at lunchtime?
The lunch-pack of Notre Dame.

Why does a baby pig eat so much?
To make a hog of himself.

What is a forum?
A two-um plus two-um.

When does the sea seem to be friendly?
When it waves.

Why is it hard to talk with a goat around?
Because he always butts in.

What kind of drivers never get arrested, however fast they go?
Screw-drivers.

What games do miners play?
Mineopoly.

What is white and dashes through the desert with a bed pan.
Florence of Arabia.

Why do birds fly south in winter?
Because it's too far to walk.

What jumps out of the ground and shouts 'Knickers'?
Crude oil.

What jumps out of the ground and shouts 'Underwear'?
Refined oil.

What's yellow and stupid?
Thick custard.

What is copper nitrate?
Overtime pay for policemen.

Why is the theatre a sad place?
Because the seats are always in tiers.

What man shaves twenty times a day?
A barber.

Why is a dentist always unhappy?
Because he looks down in the mouth.

Where do frogs fly flags?
On tadpoles.

What did the Arab say when he left his friends?
Oil see you again.

What did the Eskimo's wife sing when her husband asked her what she was cooking for supper?
Whale meat again.

What gloves can be held but not worn?
Foxgloves.

What happened to the kleptomaniac's daughter?
She took after her mother.

What did the trampoline performer say?
Life has its ups and downs, but I always bounce back.

DICTIONARY

A

Aaron - What a wig has.
Abandon - What a hat has.
Abundance - A disco in a bakery.
Accord - A thick piece of string.
Acquire - A group of singers.
Adult - A person who grows outwards instead of upwards.
Allocate - Greeting a girl named Catherine.

B

Bacteria - Rear entrance to a cafeteria.
Benign - Be a year older than eight.
Bier - A ghost's favourite drink.
Bigotry - A larger tree.
Blackmail - A letter dropped in the mud by the postman.
Broadcast - A group of plump actors.

C

Candidate - Putting small fruit in a tin.
Carpet - Animal kept for travelling.
Cartoon - Song sung in a car.
Cashew - A sneeze.

Chile - Cold country.
Choke - a very funny story.

D

Daze - Seven twenty-four-hour periods in a week.
Debate - Used for fishing.
Deceit - Four-legged piece of furniture.
Deer - A rich animal.
Deficiency - Creatures that live in the ocean.
Dentist - A boring person.
Depend - Opposite to the shallow part of the pool.
Dry dock - A thirsty surgeon.

E

Eavesdrop - Adam's wife listening to gossip.
Egg white - Snow White's brother.
Elephant - Modest animal, never seen without trunks.
Endorse - Opposite to outside.
Engineers - What engines hear with.
Europe - Piece of string belonging to you.

F

Fanfare - Exhibition of fans.
Fatso - A thin person gone to waist.
Felon - Dropped from above.
Fiddlesticks - Used to play violins with.
Flaw - Opposite to ceiling.
Fodder - Male parent.
Fungus - Man called Gus who has a good time.

G

Giraffe - Highest form of animal life.
Gnu - Opposite to old.
Good-bye - A bargain.
Gravely - How an undertaker speaks.

H

Haddock - Pain in skull

Hatchet - What a hen does with an egg.

High chair - Friendly greeting to a piece of
furniture.

Horizon - Expression used when a girl is looking at
something.

Hot dog - Canine who has sat too long by the fire.

Humphrey - Name of camel with three humps.

I

Ice cream - Cry at the top of your voice.

Ideal - What you say after shuffling a pack of cards.

Illegal - A sick bird.

Impeccable - Something chickens can't eat.

Infantry - Army for babies.

Inkling - A baby fountain pen.

Intense - Where boy scouts sleep.

J

Jargon - A missing container.

Joan of Arc - Noah's wife.

Juicy - Did you notice?

K

Kidnap - What a baby does after lunch.
Kindred - Fear of relatives.
Knotholes - Not holes.

L

Laplander - Someone unable to keep their balance on a crowded bus.
Laughing stock - Humorous cows.
Laundress - Garment used for cutting the grass.
Legalize - What a lawyer sees with.
Loving cup - Affectionate piece of china.
Lunatic - A spaceman's watch makes this sound.

M

Marigold - Someone who weds for money.
Market - What a teacher does with your homework.
Meantime - A nasty clock.
Meatball - A disco for butchers.
Melancholy - Fruit eaten by dogs.
Moonbeams - What holds the moon up.
Motel - William Tell's sister.
Myth - An unmarried moth.

N

Neurosis - Fresh flowers.
Nightingale - Very windy evening.
Normalize - Good vision.
Noticeable - See a male cow.

O

Occident - Two oxen bumping into each other.
Ohm - No place like it.
Olive - Where you reside.
Operator - Person who dislikes operas.
Orangeade - Help for fruit.
Ouch - Sound made by two hedgehogs kissing.

P

Panther - Person who makes panths.
Peephole - A group of human beings.
Pharmacist - Someone who helps on a farm.
Picket - Select something.
Piggy bank - Where pigs keep money.
Pink carnation - Country where all the cars are pink.
Poker - What you do to a donkey to get her to move.
Prehistoric times - Stone Age newspaper.

Q

Quack - Doctor who treats sick ducks.

Quartz - Four to the gallon.
Quota - Repeating what a lady said.

R

Radioactive - A busy wireless.
Ragtime - When your clothes wear out.
Ramshackle - Handcuff for male sheep.
Rash prediction - You will have chicken pox.
Refuse - Something that has to be done when the lights go out.
Revolving door - Place to go around with people.
Rocket - What a mother does to get her baby to sleep.

S

Safety - Refreshment that isn't dangerous.
Sarong - Expression used by a teacher when your work is incorrect.
Seafarer - Someone who collects the money on a ship.
Senile - Visit to Egypt's famous river.
Shooting star - Actor who plays cowboys.
Sneakers - Shoes worn by cats to chase mice.
Sourpuss - Cat that eats lemons.
Sturgeon - Fish doctor.

T

Taint - Is not.
Tannery - Place for sunbathing.
Temper - The only thing you can lose and still have.
Toadstool - Seat for frogs.
Tortoise - What the teacher did.
Tulips - What you kiss with.

U

Unit - Term of abuse.
Urchin - Lower part of a woman's face.
Urgent - Her boyfriend.

V

Variegate - Choice of entrances.
Vertigo - Question asked when someone sets out on a journey.
Viscount - Requesting Violet to add up.

W

Wagging tail - A happy ending.
Waltz - Something that belongs to Walter.
Wholesale - Sale of holes.

Whose - Where a Scotsman lives.

X

X - What hens lay.
Xerophyte - Is there an argument?
X-ray - Belly vision.

Y

Yank - How an American dentist draws teeth.
Yearnings - What you receive for working.
Yokel - Someone who laughs at yokes.

Z

Zeus - Where animals are kept in cages.
Zinc - Place for washing up.
Zuider Zee - On the coast.

MORE KNOCK-KNOCKS

Knock, knock.
Who's there?
Sabina.
Sabina who?
Sabina long time since I saw you.

Knock, knock,
Who's there?
Mischa.
Mischa who?
Mischa a lot while you've been away.

Knock, knock.
Who's there?
Dishwasher.
Dishwasher who?
Dishwasher the way I spoke before I had false
teeth.

Knock, knock.
Knock, knock.
Ring, ring.
Who's there?
U.C.I.
U.C.I. who?
U.C.I. had to ring, because you didn't answer when
I knocked.

Knock, knock.
Who's there?
Ivor.
Ivor who?
Ivor sore hand from knocking at this door.

Knock, knock.
Who's there?
Ida.
Ida who?
Ida know. Sorry.

Knock, knock.
Who's there?
Ida, again.
Ida who?
Ida terrible time remembering who I was.

Knock, knock.
Who's there?
Ken.
Ken who?
Ken I come in? It's freezing out here!

Knock, knock.
Who's there?
Martin.
Martin who?
Martin of beans won't open.

Knock, knock.
Who's there?
Atch.
Atch who?
Bless you. Didn't know you had a cold.

Knock, knock.
Who's there?
Jemima.
Jemima who?
Jemima asking whose house this is?

Knock, knock.
Who's there?
Ivor.
Ivor who?
Ivor message for you.

Knock, knock.
Who's there?
Ivor.
Ivor who?
Ivor good mind not to tell you.

Knock, knock.
Who's there?
Bella.
Bella who?
Bella no ringa, thatsa why I knocka.

Knock, knock.
Who's there?
Jewel.
Jewel who?
Jewel remember when you see my face.

Knock, knock.
Who's there?
N.E.
N.E. who?
N.E. body you like, as long as you let me in.

Knock, knock.
Who's there?
You.
You who?
Yoo-hoo! Anyone at home?

Knock, knock.
Who's there?
Granny.
Knock, knock.
Who's there?
Granny.
Knock, knock.
Who's there?
Granny.
Knock, knock.
Who's there?
Aunt.
Aunt who?
Aunt you glad I got rid of all those grannies?

Knock, knock.
Who's there?
Mahatma.
Mahatma who?
Mahatma coat please.

Knock, knock.
Who's there?
Cattle.
Cattle who?
Cattle always purr if you stroke it.

Knock, knock.
Who's there?
Dummy.
Dummy who?
Dummy a favour and get lost.

Knock, knock.
Who's there?
Ammonia.
Ammonia who?
Ammonia little boy, come and let me in.

Knock, knock.
Who's there?
Fozzie.
Fozzie who?
Fozzie hundredth time my name is Paul.

Knock, knock.
Who's there?
A little old lady.
A little old lady who?
I didn't know you could yodel.

Knock, knock.
Who's there?
Ivan.
Ivan who?
Ivan infectious disease.
SLAM!

Knock, knock.
Who's there?
Solly.
Solly who?
Solly you've been tloubled. Me makee mistakee.

Knock, knock.
Who's there?
Wooden shoe.
Wooden shoe who?
Wooden shoe like to know!

Knock, knock.
Who's there?
Percy.
Percy who?
Percyvere and you may find out.

Knock, knock.
Who's there?
Yvonne.
Yvonne who?
Yvonne to be alone.

Knock, knock.
Who's there?
Ewan.
Ewan who?
No, just you and me.

Knock, knock.
Who's there?
Cows.
Cows who?
No, cows go moo, not who.

Knock, knock.
Who's there?
Butcher.
Butcher who?
Butcher arms around me, honey, hold me tight ...

Knock, knock.
Who's there?
Mr.
Mr. Who?
Mr. bus home, that's why I'm late.

Knock, knock.
Who's there?
Hugo.
Hugo who?
Hugo that way, and I'll go this.

Knock, knock.
Who's there?
Colin.
Colin who?
Colin the doctor, I don't feel well.

Knock, knock.
Who's there?
Ketchup.
Ketchup who?
Ketchup with me and I'll tell you.

Knock, knock.
Who's there?
Huron.
Huron who?
Huron time for once.

Knock, knock.
Who's there?
Noise.
Noise who?
Noise to see you after all this time.

Knock, knock.
Who's there?
Olivia.
Olivia who?
Olivia, but I've forgotten my key.

Knock, knock.
Who's there?
Water.
Water who?
Water be ashamed of yourself, living in a dump like this.

Knock, knock.
Who's there?
Cook.
Cook who?
That's the first one I've heard this year.

Knock, knock.
Who's there?
Luke.
Luke who?
Luke through the keyhole and you'll see.

Knock, knock.
Who's there?
Musket.
Musket who?
Musket in, I'm in a hurry.

Knock, knock.
Who's there?
Scot.
Scot who?
Scot absolutely nothing to do with you.

Knock, knock.
Who's there?
Alec.
Alec who?
Alec you very much indeed.

Knock, knock.
Who's there?
Four eggs.
Four eggs who?
Four eggsample, open the door.

Knock, knock.
Who's there?
Nadia.
Nadia who?
Nadia head examined if you understand what I'm saying.

Knock, knock.
Who's there?
Arthur.
Arthur who?
Arthur any more at home like you?

Knock, knock.
Who's there?
Zsa Zsa.
Zsa Zsa who?
Zsa Zsa last knock, knock joke I want to hear.

Knock, knock.
Who's there?
Viola.
Viola who?
Viola sudden you not know me?

Knock, knock.
Who's there?
Euripedes.
Euripedes who?
Euripedes and you'll not get a new pair.

Knock, knock.
Who's there?
Major.
Major who?
Major answer the door, didn't I!

Knock, knock.
Who's there?
Ali.
Ali who?
Alleluyah, you opened the door.

Knock, knock.
Who's there?
Ann.
Ann who?
Ann apple just fell on my head.

Knock, knock.
Who's there?
Toodle.
Toodle who?
Ta ta!

A LIBRARY
OF LAUGHS

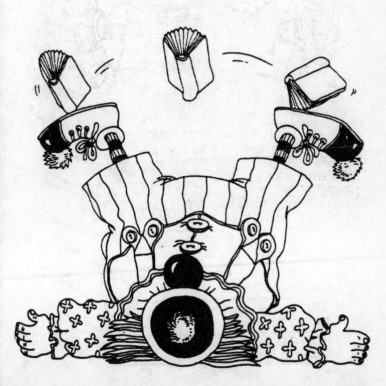

62 GREAT BOOK TITLES
(not recommended for reading)

A GOOD READ
by Ann Ortha

IS IT LOVE?
by Midas Wellbe

I LOVE SWEETS
by Oliver Nutherwon

EAGER GIRL
by May I. Help

HIDE AND SEEK
by I. C. Hugh

OFF TO MARKET
by Tobias A. Pigg

THE EMPTY TANK
by Phil R. Upp

DESERT CROSSING
by I. Rhoda Camel

THE WINNER
by Vic Tree

1066
by Norman Invasion

THE ANGRY LION
by Claudia Armoff

THE BIG PARTY
by Maud D. Merrier

I WANT TO MEET YOU
by Tamara Knight

WHO KILLED COCK ROBIN?
by Howard I. Know

HOW TO AVOID ARGUMENTS
by Xavier Breath

TEN YEARS IN THE APE HOUSE
by Bab Boone

HOW TO FALL OUT OF A WINDOW
by Eileen Dover

SAD WOMAN
by Paul Aidy

HIDE AND SEEK
by I. C. You

A HOLE IN MY ROOF
by Lee King

AGAINST THE LAW
by Kermit A. Crime

THE WRONG SHOE
by Titus Canbe

THE SHORT BREAK
by T. N. Biscuits

SAY YOUR PRAYERS
by Neil Down

WHO SAW HIM LEAVE
by Wendy Go

THE BROKEN WINDOW
by Eva Brick

THE PAINTER
by R. T. Stick

THE DRUNKARD
by Carrie Mehome

THE HOUSING PROBLEM
by Rufus Quick

THE WELSH COMEDIAN
by Dai Larfin

THE UNEMPLOYED MAGICIAN
by Trixie Coulden-Doo

DETECTIVE STORIES
by Watts E. Dunn

IT'S A HOLD UP
by Nick R. Elastic

THE MATCH ON THE GRASS
by Lorna Light

HOW TO BE A MILLIONAIRE
by Ivor Lott

THE SUBURBS
by Bill Tupperalot

OLD FURNITURE
by Ann Teak

WHICH WAY OUT?
by Isadora Negsitt

IN THE COUNTRY
by Theresa Greene

TUG OF WAR
by Paul Hard

CERTAINTY
by R. U. Sure

CENTRAL HEATING
by Ray D. Ater

EMPTY PETROL TANK
by Phil Arrup

LONG WALK
by Miss D. Bus

SLEEP
by Annie Stethic

THE GREAT ESCAPE
by Freda Convict

SORRY NOT POSSIBLE
by Fred I. Cant

CHRISTMAS PLANTS
by Miss L. Toe

THE HAUNTED HOUSE
by Hugo First

COOKING EQUIPMENT
by U. Tensils

MAKE MONEY QUICKLY
by Rob. A. Bank

HORRIBLE HOWLERS

HOWL!

'What is a sick joke?'
'Something you mustn't bring up in polite company.'

'Mummy, why can't we get a waste disposal unit?'
'Keep quiet and get chewing.'

A gladiator to his friend, facing the lions in Ancient
Rome:
'One thing, you don't get hooligans running across
the pitch.'

What should you do when you see Dracula,
Frankenstein's monster, four werewolfs, two
vampires and the Incredible Hulk all in one room?
Keep your fingers crossed and hope that it's a fancy
dress party.

Why did the monster give up boxing?
He didn't want to spoil his looks.

Why do demons and ghouls get on so well?
Because demons are a ghoul's best friend.

'But I don't want to go to Australia, mummy.'
'Shut up, and keep swimming.'

What is a monster's favourite soup?
Scream of tomato.

'Mummy, mummy, what's a vampire?'
'Shut up, and drink your soup before it clots.'

What did the vampire say after his visit to the
dentist?
'Fangs very much.'

I used to be a werewolf, but I'm alright
nowoooooooooooooooh!'

What do monsters do every night at 11 o'clock?
Take a coffin break.

'Mum, there's a woman outside with a pram.'
'Well, tell her to push off.'

Little Audrey was out walking one day with her
grandmother. Road workers were busy mending
the road and there were lorries and steamrollers all
over the place. Suddenly Audrey's grandmother
spotted a coin in the road.
   'Look a 50p piece!' she shouted and ran straight
out into the road to pick it up.
   Just as she bent down a steamroller came around
the corner and squashed her flat as a pancake.
   Little Audrey laughed and laughed; she knew all
along that it wasn't a 50p piece, but only a 10p.

'Mum, there's a man outside collecting for the Old
Folks Home.
'Well, give him grannie.'

'What did the monster eat after his teeth had been
pulled out?'
'The dentist.'

Cannibal Wife: I don't know what to make of my husband.
Friend: How about a hotpot?

'Excuse me, your wife just fell in that well!'
'That's okay, nobody drinks water from there anymore.'

Count Dracula has denied that he is to marry the Viscountess Vampire.
They remain just good friends.

Here's your chance to join the Dracula Fan Club - just send your name, address, and blood sample to …

1st Ghost: I find haunting castles a bore these days.
2nd Ghost: Me too. I don't seem to be able to put any life into it anymore.

What sort of meat does Dracula hate?
Steak.

A man stood on a bridge one night,
His lips were all a quiver.
He gave a cough,
His leg fell off,
And floated down the river.

How did the dentist become a brain surgeon?
His drill slipped.

Mark: I hear you play golf, what do you usually go around in?
Peter: Oh, I usually wear a sweater.

'Excuse me, but you look like Helen Green.'
'So what, I look awful in pink too.'

A man went to some stables and saw a beautiful horse which he decided he would like to buy. He bargained with the animal's owner and eventually bought the horse for a considerable sum.

The man jumped on the horse and shouted:
'Giddyup!' but the horse didn't move a muscle.

The dealer explained that it was a very special horse and that it would only move if you said: 'Praise the Lord' to it. And to stop it you simply had to say 'Amen'.

Bearing this in mind the man cried: 'Praise the Lord!' at the top of his voice, at which the horse took off at a very great speed and headed towards a cliff.

The man was alarmed, and only just remembered in time to shout 'Amen!' at which the horse screeched to a halt right at the very edge of the cliff.

Feeling much relieved when he saw the one hundred metre drop below, the rider raised his eyes to heaven and exclaimed: 'Praise the Lord'.

Psychiatrist: Congratulations, Mr Young. You're finally cured of your delusion. But why are you so sad?

Patient: Wouldn't you be sad if yesterday you were the King of England and the next day you were nobody.

Wife: Wake up! Wake up! There's a burglar in the kitchen and he's eating the stew left over from supper!

Husband: Go back to sleep. I'll bury him in the morning.

Father: What are you looking for, Harold?
Harold: I'm looking for a 50p piece.
Father: Where did you lose this 50p piece?
Harold: Oh, I didn't lose it. I'm just looking for one.

'Our hen can lay an egg six centimetres long. Can you beat that?'
'Yes, with an egg beater.'

What was said to Emillion when he did someone a good turn?
Thanks Emillion.

Editor: Did you write about Lord Nelson?
Young reporter: Yes, boss.
Editor: How much space did you give him?
Young reporter: Oh, a whole column to himself.

'Doctor, doctor, I feel like a horse.'
'How long have you felt like this?'
'Ever since I won the 2.30 at Epsom.'

Two flies were sitting on Robinson Crusoe's knee.
'Goodbye,' said one, 'I'll see you on Friday.'

Teacher: Potts! You're three hours late for school and you only live just around the corner. What took you so long to get here?
Pupil: I had to say goodbye to my pets before I left for school.
Teacher: How long does it take to say goodbye to a cat, a dog and a goldfish?
Pupil: But, sir, I have an ant farm.

Visitor: Is this a healthy place to live?
Local man: Definitely. When I came here I couldn't take any solid food, and I couldn't walk. Now look at me.
Visitor: What was wrong with you?
Local man: Nothing. I was born here.

'I'm going to study singing.'
'Good. A long way away I hope.'

Morris: I once saw a magician turn a rabbit into a dove.
Doris: So what, I once saw a magician walk down a street and turn into a shop.

'You mean they put you in prison just because you were making big money?'
'That's right - about an inch too big.'

John: Why did you become a bus driver?
Dave: So that I could tell people where to get off.

A girl went to visit her grandmother. The grandmother was distressed by what she considered was her granddaughter's slovenly speech and decided that she must speak to her about it.

'My dear,' she said, 'there are just two words that I wish you wouldn't use quite so often. One is "great" and the other is "lousy"'.

'Certainly grandma,' said the girl, 'what are they?'

Alice: You'd be a good dancer but for two things.
Terry: What are they?
Alice: Your feet.

Simple Simon: Why are you walking along with one foot on the pavement and one foot on the road.

Smart Alec: Am I? Thank goodness for that, I thought I'd got a limp.

A man and a woman were sitting on the river bank, both dangling their legs in the water. Suddenly a crocodile swam towards them, snapped its jaws and bit off one of the man's feet.

'Help,' shouted the man. 'A crocodile's just bitten off one of my feet!'

'Which one?' asked his friend.

'I don't know, all crocodiles look alike to me.'

Mother: Doctor, last summer my son became convinced he was a bullfrog.
Psychiatrist: But this is winter, why have you waited so long before coming to see me?
Mother: I couldn't afford it.
Psychiatrist: How can you afford it now?
Mother: Well, thanks to my son I saved a fortune last summer on flyspray and insect killers.

'Does your sister still make up jokes?'
'Yes, she's still got that job in the beauty parlour.'

Optician: Can you read the chart on the wall.
Patient: What wall?

'My father wrote a book called *How to Avoid Paying Taxes*.'
'Is he writing another book?'
'Yes, it's called *My Life in Wormwood Scrubs*.'

A visitor was marooned in a town because of a landslide caused by very heavy rain, which was still falling in torrents after three days. Looking out of the window of a restaurant he remarked to the waitress:

'This is like the Flood.'

'The what?' she replied.

'The Flood. Surely you've heard of the Flood and Noah's Ark?'

'No, mister,' said the waitress, 'I haven't seen a newspaper for days.'

What do you call someone who steals your beer? Nick McGuinness.

Did you hear about the magician who sawed a lady in half?
She's in hospital - Wards 5 and 6.

Father: Look, I told you before, I'm not going to buy you a set of drums.

Duncan: But Dad, I promise I'll only play them while you're sleeping.

A tramp knocked on the door of a doctor's house and the door was opened by a very attractive young lady.

'Excuse me,' said the tramp. 'Do you think the doctor would be willing to part with any old clothes, so that a poor old tramp won't feel the cold this winter?'

'I'm sure the doctor is perfectly willing,' said the young lady, 'but I really don't think they would suit you. I'm the doctor.'

'I'm so sorry, madam, I just ran over your cat. I'd like to replace it.'
'Very well, but how good are you at catching mice?'

A man was charged with robbing a jewellers' and wanted a top lawyer to defend him in court.

'I'll handle your case,' said the lawyer, 'If you swear to me that you are innocent and pay my fee of £300.'

The crook thought for a minute and said:

'Will you do it for £100, a gold watch and some pearl earrings?'

Newspaper Reporter:	I've got a big scoop.
Editor:	What is it?
Reporter:	The council have just bought a mechanical shovel.

Jimmy: What did Dr Watson say to Sherlock Holmes in 1906?

Timmy: I haven't a clue.

'Mr Rembrandt, do you ever paint people in the nude?'
'Certainly not! I always wear clothes when I paint.'

HORROR STORIES

What do you get if you cross a midget with
Dracula?
A vampire that sucks blood from your kneecaps.

What happens when monsters hold a beauty
contest?
Nobody wins.

Who is murderous and comes from the fishmonger?
Jack the Kipper.

RUDE JOKE RUDE JOKE RUDE JOKE RUDE JOKE RUDE JOKE RUDE JOKE RUDE
Willie with a thirst for gore,
Nailed his sister to the door;
Mother said with humour quaint:
'Now, Willie dear, don't scratch the paint.'
RUDE JOKE RUDE JOKE RUDE JOKE RUDE JOKE RUDE JOKE RUDE JOKE RUDE

MOTHER ON BEACH: Children, tell me where
  you've buried your father. He's got the train
  tickets home.

What happened to the undertaker when he retired?
He went and buried himself in the country.

'Doctor, doctor, I keep thinking I'm a ghost.'
'I wondered why you just walked through the wall.'

How does a worried skeleton look?
Grave.

Why are vampire families close?
Because blood is thicker than water.

Why did the vampire actress turn down so many film offers?
She was waiting for a part that she could get her teeth into.

MONSTER MOTHER: How many times do I have to tell you not to eat with your fingers? Use the spade like I taught you.

1ST MONSTER: That girl over there just rolled her eyes at me.

2ND MONSTER: Well roll them back, she might need them.

MOTHER MONSTER: Don't sit in that chair; it's for Rigor Mortis to set in.

What happened to the girl who slept with her head under the pillow?
The fairies took all her teeth out.

Why did the Cyclops give up teaching?
He only had one pupil.

What did the skeleton say to his girlfriend?
'I love every bone in your body.'

What does a monster do when he loses a hand?
He goes to a second-hand shop.

What is big, green and smells?
A monster's bottom.

Why are ghosts simple things?
Because you can see right through them.

Which monster made friends with the three bears?
Ghouldilocks.

What did Frankenstein's monster say when he was
struck by lightning?
'That was just what I needed.'

Where does the Bride of Frankenstein have her hair done?
At the ugly parlour.

How did Frankenstein's monster eat its food?
It bolted it down.

Why is the graveyard such a noisy place?
Because of the coffin.

'What's the death rate around here?'
'Same as everywhere else. One death per person.'

EMBARRASSING MOMENTS

Holy! Holy! Holy!

Get an adult to punch a hole in the middle of an old teaspoon for you. A plastic teaspoon will be perfectly all right. Place the spoon in a bowl of sugar and wait for one of your guests to spoon some sugar into their tea. How embarrassing when sugar pours through the hole all over the place!

It's Going Round

The next time somebody rides past you on a bicycle, point to the back wheel and shout:
    'Your back wheel's touching the ground!'
Your unfortunate victim will almost certainly get off the bike and stop to have a look at the back wheel! It also works if you shout:
    'Your front wheel's going round!'
When they realise that they have been very silly, they can't accuse you of anything - after all, you have only spoken the truth.

Long Jump

Try this on your friends:
YOU: I bet you I can jump across the street.
VICTIM: I bet you can't.
YOU: I bet you £100 I can.
VICTIM: I bet you £100 you can't!
YOU: OK then.
You then very carefully cross the road, and when you are standing across the street, you jump!

Rude Balloons

Take an ordinary balloon. Blow some air into it, but do not tie the neck. Instead, let the air out very slowly, pulling the neck as you do so.

You will discover that as the air escapes from the balloon it will make some extremely funny and sometimes rude noises. Try it a few times, letting the air out slowly, then very quickly, and you will find that you can make a whole variety of noises. Choose the one you like best, or the one that is the rudest, and practise it.

Now, with the balloon hidden behind your back, let the air out and make the rude noise when people are least expecting it - at the bus stop, in the supermarket, or during school assembly!

Black Mark

Borrow some of your mother's or sister's dark eye-shadow. You are not going to put it on your eyelids though; instead put a little on your finger.

Now tell a friend that she has a black mark on the side of her nose. Tell her to stand still and you will wipe it off. You pretend to wipe away the smudge that isn't there, but actually put one on!

Your friend will go off feeling happy that you have wiped an embarrassing mark away, not realising how funny you have made her look!

Keep Your Eyes Open

YOU: You'd better keep your eyes open tomorrow.
VICTIM: Why?
YOU: Otherwise you'll bump into things.

Kiss The Book

YOU: Do you see this book?

VICTIM: Yes, why?

YOU: I bet you that I can kiss it inside and outside without even opening it.

VICTIM: I bet you can't.

YOU: I bet I can!

All you do is kiss the book on the cover, then take it outside and kiss it again. You have kissed it inside and out and you haven't opened it up!

Warning!

YOU: Look out! There's a henweigh on your back.

VICTIM: What's a henweigh?

YOU: Oh, about three pounds.

How Dreadful!

The very next time you are on a crowded bus or train with a friend, and are standing in a crush because there aren't enough seats to go round, suddenly say to your friend:

'Do you realise that your trousers/skirt have just fallen down?'

Ahhhh! Screaaaaam! If the bus is very crowded they won't even be able to look down to see if it is true!

RUDE JOKE RUDE JOKE RUDE JOKE RUDE JOKE RUDE JOKE RUDE JOKE RUDE

What would you do?

YOU: If you were walking down a very narrow country lane, which had no trees to climb and no holes to hide in and you didn't have a gun and there wasn't a soul about to help you, and you saw a great fierce grizzly bear coming towards you, what would you do?

VICTIM: Run.

YOU: What, with a bear behind?!

RUDE JOKE RUDE JOKE RUDE JOKE RUDE JOKE RUDE JOKE RUDE JOKE RUDE

Droopy drawers!

To give someone a surprise when they open their
drawers, simply take out the top drawer of a chest
of drawers or dressing table. Carefully remove
everything that is inside the drawer and store it in a
box for safe-keeping. Turn the drawer upside down
so that the bottom of the drawer is now at the top,
and put it back where it came from.

When your victim opens the drawer to put
something inside they will feel very silly when they
find that they can't get their hand inside the
drawer.

RIOTOUS RIDDLES

RUDE JOKE RUDE JOKE RUDE JOKE RUDE JOKE RUDE JOKE RUDE JOKE RUDE

Why did the lobster blush?
Because the sea weed.

RUDE JOKE RUDE JOKE RUDE JOKE RUDE JOKE RUDE JOKE RUDE JOKE RUDE

Why does lightning shock people?
Because it doesn't know how to conduct itself.

Why wasn't Eve afraid of catching measles?
Because she'd Adam.

How many sheep does it take to make one pullover?
Sheep can't knit, you fool!

Who has more fun when you tickle a mule?
The mule might enjoy it, but you'll get the biggest kick out of it.

When an apple hits a banana in the mouth, what is it called?
A fruit punch.

What has a neck and a bottom but no arms or legs?
A bottle.

Why are elephants so rude?
Because when they go swimming they only have one pair of trunks between two.

What is black, white and red?
A skunk with nappy rash.

RUDE JOKE RUDE JOKE RUDE JOKE RUDE JOKE RUDE JOKE RUDE JOKE RUDE
What do you do when your nose goes on strike?
Picket.
RUDE JOKE RUDE JOKE RUDE JOKE RUDE JOKE RUDE JOKE RUDE JOKE RUDE

What do you get when your head is chopped off?
A splitting headache.

What is a sausage?
A hamburger in tights.

What sits in a fruit bowl and shouts for help?
A damson in distress.

212

Why can't a steam engine sit down?
Because it has a tender behind.

What do you get if you cross the Atlantic with the Titanic?
Halfway.

What did the traffic light say to the zebra crossing?
Don't look now, I'm changing.

What do you call two comedians that cure indigestion?
The Two Rennies.

What is green and swings through trees?
A septic monkey.

What do koalas take on holiday?
The bear essentials.

Who invented vulgar fractions?
Henry the $1/8$.

What did the violin say to the harp?
May I string along with you?

What fur did Adam and Eve wear?
Bearskins.

What is yellow and smells of bananas?
A monkey that's been sick.

What did one wall say to the other wall?
I'll meet you at the corner.

What did one eye say to the other eye?
There's something between us that smells.

A pupil was late for school one day. The teacher
was just about to scold the boy, when she thought
that she had better first find out if he had a good
reason.

'Yes, my father got burnt this morning.'

'Oh, how awful,' said the teacher looking
shocked. 'I hope it wasn't too serious?'

'Serious?' said the boy. 'They don't mess about at
that crematorium.'

* * *

A young man started his first job as a door-to-door
brush salesman, selling every possible kind of
brush imaginable. His first assignment was in the
country and he called at a very remote cottage. He
knocked at the door and a little old lady answered
the door. She hadn't very much money and

however hard the young man tried, he simple couldn't persuade her to buy anything. He was just about to go when suddenly he thought of a smaller and cheaper brush that he had - a lavatory brush. He showed it to the old lady and she seemed very interested. To his surprise she bought one.

A year later the man was back in the country again and called at the same cottage. Remembering the lavatory brush he asked the old lady about it and how she had got on with it.

'Well, I like it very much,' said the old lady, 'but my husband hates it. He's so old fashioned he still prefers using toilet paper.'

* * *

A Norfolk butcher was famous for his rabbit pies, which he used to bake himself. As time went by, however, customers started to complain that his pies weren't quite as nice as they used to be. One day a friend said:

'Horace, what's happened to your rabbit pies?'

'Why?'

'They don't taste like they used to.'

'Well between you and me,' said the butcher, 'my pies have been in such great demand that there aren't enough rabbits to go round.'

'So what do you do?'

'I mix in a bit of horse meat.'

'Horse meat!' exclaimed the friend. 'How much horse meat do you put in?'

'About fifty-fifty,' replied the butcher.

'What do you mean fifty:fifty?'

'One horse to one rabbit.'

* * *

Ronald Peabody was rushed to hospital one day with acute appendicitis. As an emergency case he was taken straight to the operating theatre. Mrs Peabody had been out shopping, but as soon as she heard the news she hurried to the hospital, and said to the receptionist:

'Where's my Ronald?'

'Who?' asked the amazed receptionist.

'Ronald Peabody! Where is he?'

'Well he's in the operating theatre at this very moment. Dr Killjoy is performing the surgery.'

'Who's Dr Killjoy?' demanded the wife. 'I'm not having any strange man opening my male!'

* * *

A doctor was doing his weekly rounds at a lunatic asylum. One particular patient seemed to be much improved and the doctor told him that he would see him again on Wednesday, and if he was just as well he would be allowed out. The doctor left the asylum and was just unlocking the door of his car when a brick hit him on the back of the head. As he lay on the ground he saw the patient leaning out of a window, shouting: 'Don't forget Wednesday!'

* * *

Old Mr and Mrs Jenkins used to argue terribly. They didn't like the same food, the same furniture, anything. After one almighty row Mr Jenkins walked out of the house and slammed the door so hard that a painting shot off the wall.

He stayed away for twenty years, until one day he turned up on the doorstep.

'And where have you been?' shouted his wife.

'None of your business!' he shouted back.

'Well pick up that painting and let's not be having any more of your nonsense!'

* * *

Little Sally was very fond of her little cat called Paddy. They were inseparable and the only time they were apart was when little Sally was at school. Sadly, one morning while Sally was at school, Paddy ran out into the road and was knocked down by a car and killed.

Sally's mother was very distressed and didn't know how she was going to break the awful news. She went along to the school and waited outside the gates. When Sally appeared, her mother said:

'You must be a brave little girl. Something dreadful has happened. Little Paddy has been run over and killed.'

The girl shrugged her shoulders and asked:

'What's for tea tonight; I'm starving?'

'Didn't you hear me?' asked the mother, 'Paddy is dead.' Little Sally burst into tears and began sobbing her heart out. Through her tears she said:

'I thought you said Daddy.'

* * *

Letter from a schoolgirl:

Dear Auntie Constance,
The school did *Hamlet* last week. Most of the parents had seen it before, but they laughed just the same …

DARING DAUGHTERS

MOTHER: And what did you study at school today?
DAUGHTER: All kinds of things, but mostly gozinta.
MOTHER: What on earth's that? A new kind of language?
DAUGHTER: No, two gozinta four, four gozinta eight …

MOTHER: How was your first day at school, Lizzie?
LIZZIE: OK, but it was spoilt by some woman that we have to call 'Miss'. She ruined everything.

GHOUL FRIEND: My goodness, hasn't your little ghoul grown!
GHOUL MOTHER: Yes, she's certainly gruesome.

AUNT MILDRED: And what are you going to give your brother for his birthday?
NANCY: I don't know. Last year I gave him chicken pox.

MOTHER: Why have you come home from school early?
DAUGHTER: Because of sickness.
MOTHER: Why, have you been ill?
DAUGHTER: No, it was the teacher. She got sick of me.

AGNES: Mum, you know that vase you were always worried I would break?
MOTHER: Yes, dear.
AGNES: Well, your worries are over.

MOTHER: Do you like your new English teacher?
GILLIAN: No, he's so biased.
MOTHER: Why is he so biased?
GILLIAN: He thinks words can only be spelt one
  way.

RUDE JOKE RUDE JOKE RUDE JOKE RUDE JOKE RUDE JOKE RUDE JOKE RUDE

SYBIL: Mum, I think the dog is feeling
  uncomfortable.
MOTHER: What makes you say that?
SYBIL: He just leaked the information.

RUDE JOKE RUDE JOKE RUDE JOKE RUDE JOKE RUDE JOKE RUDE JOKE RUDE

ANNIE: My mum struck it rich the other day.
LILY: Did she win the pools?
ANNIE: No, she drove the car straight into a bank.

The baker's daughter Lucy Jones
Has lots and lots of fun,
For every time she does her hair
She puts it in a bun.

What's the difference between a girl who's smart,
and a girl who decides to do something?
One minds her make-up, the other makes her mind up.

MARY: Is it correct to say that you water your horse?
MOTHER: Yes.
MARY: Then I'm just going to milk the cat.

Which burn longer - the candles on a boy's birthday cake or the candles on a girl's birthday cake?
Neither - all candles burn shorter.

MOTHER: What are you doing with my best fur-lined boots?
SANDRA: Well, you wouldn't want me to get your new silk slippers wet, would you?

TANIA: Mummy, we're going to play a game of elephants. Will you play with us?
MOTHER: Yes, dear. What do I have to do?
TANIA: We pretend to be elephants, and you feed us peanuts and sticky buns.

RUDE JOKE RUDE JOKE RUDE JOKE RUDE JOKE RUDE JOKE RUDE JOKE RUDE
'Mummy, does God use our bathroom?'
'No dear, why?'
'Because every morning Daddy bangs on the bathroom door and shouts, "Oh God, are you still in there!"'
RUDE JOKE RUDE JOKE RUDE JOKE RUDE JOKE RUDE JOKE RUDE JOKE RUDE

SYLVIA: What nationality are you?
MERYL: Mother was born in Iceland and father was born in Cuba, so I suppose I'm an ice cube.

A little girl was in a petshop with her mother when she noticed a cage of green parakeets.
'Oh look, Mum,' said the little girl, 'there are some canaries that aren't ripe.'

220

Little Edna was taking her dog for a walk, when she was stopped by a policeman.

'Do you have a licence for that dog?' he asked.

'Oh no,' said little Edna. 'He's not old enough to drive yet.'

APRIL: Mother, if we sold our school teacher
would we make a lot of money?
MOTHER: I shouldn't think so, darling. Why?
APRIL: It says in this magazine that Old Masters
can be sold for a fortune.

EVIL SONS

SON: Dad, how do you spell 'High'?
FATHER: H-I-G-H. Why, what is your essay about?
SON: High-enas.

MOTHER: Have you said your prayers, Nigel?
NIGEL: Yes, Mummy.
MOTHER: What did you pray for?
NIGEL: I prayed for Rochdale to be in Devon.
MOTHER: Why? Rochdale is in Lancashire; why did you pray for it to be in Devon?
NIGEL: Because that's what I put in my geography test.

MOTHER: What did your father say about your school report?
THOMAS: Shall I leave out the bad language?
MOTHER: Yes, of course.
THOMAS: He didn't say anything.

FATHER: Well, son, there's one good thing about your school report.
SON: What's that, Dad?
FATHER: You're certainly not a cheat, otherwise you would never have got such low marks.

'Are you chewing gum?'
'No, I'm Adrian Brown.'

BILLY: How did your father break his leg?
BOBBY: He trod on his cigarette to put it out.
BILLY: How did he break his leg doing that?
BOBBY: He dropped it in an open manhole, then
stepped on it.

'I hear your son is a writer. Does he write for
money?'
'Yes, every time he writes a letter home.'

ANGRY MAN: I'll teach you to throw stones at my
greenhouse!
SCHOOLBOY: I wish you would; I keep missing.

MRS NOGGS: My son Danny will soon have to start thinking about getting a job.
MRS BOGGS: Does he have any particular leaning for anything?
MRS NOGGS: At present it's only on walls and lamp-posts.

MOTHER: Joseph, you're not supposed to eat with your knife.
JOSEPH: But, mum, my fork leaks!

ALFRED: My dog doesn't eat meat.
ALBERT: Why not?
ALFRED: I never give him any!

MAURICE: I had a parrot for a year and it never said one word.
HORACE: Maybe it was tongue-tied.
MAURICE: No, it was stuffed.

RUDE JOKE RUDE JOKE RUDE JOKE RUDE JOKE RUDE JOKE RUDE JOKE RUDE

LITTLE BOY (in church): Mummy, Mummy, I feel sick.
MOTHER: Well go to the back of the church and get some fresh air; you'll feel better then.
Ten minutes later:
MOTHER: Do you feel better now?
LITTLE BOY: Yes, there was a box at the back of the church which said 'For the Sick'.

RUDE JOKE RUDE JOKE RUDE JOKE RUDE JOKE RUDE JOKE RUDE JOKE RUDE

'I say, your son has a fine head.'
'Yes, it's as good as new. Never been used.'

JOHN: Why do elephants paint their toenails red?
MARK: I don't know; why?
JOHN: So that they can hide in the strawberry field.
MARK: I don't believe that.
JOHN: Have you ever seen an elephant in a strawberry field?
MARK: No.
JOHN: You see, it works!

'What's on the television tonight, son?'
'Same as always, Dad - a vase of flowers and a photo of grandma.'

RUDE JOKE RUDE JOKE RUDE JOKE RUDE JOKE RUDE JOKE RUDE JOKE RUDE
FATHER: What would you like for Christmas, son?
SON: I've got my eye on a new racing bike.
FATHER: Well, keep your eye on it, 'cos you'll never get your bum on it.
RUDE JOKE RUDE JOKE RUDE JOKE RUDE JOKE RUDE JOKE RUDE JOKE RUDE

TEACHER: Did someone do your homework for you?
PUPIL: My father.
TEACHER: Really? Because it's all wrong.
PUPIL: Well, I helped him with it.

JEFF: My dad threatens to strap me every time I'm naughty.

JOE: Does he ever do it?

JEFF: No, because when he takes his belt off his trousers fall down.

BOY (*to yachtsman*): What do you do when you have to contend with a lot of wind?

YACHTSMAN: I usually take indigestion tablets.

SICK STORIES

'Doctor, Doctor, you gave my wife arsenic instead of sleeping powder.'
'Oh, I'm awfully sorry. That'll be another £1.50.'

'I just don't know what to make of my husband.'
'How about a curry?'

EXECUTIONER (*to victim with head on the block*):
  'Sorry about this, but they do say third time lucky!'

What do you call a man with a spade through his head?
Doug.

What do you call a man without a spade through his head?
Douglas.

A cannibal came home and found his wife chopping up a cobra and a small native. 'Oh, no,' he said, 'not snake and pygmy pie again.'

There was once a young cannibal called Fred
Who used to eat garlic in bed.
His mother said, 'Sonny,
That's not very funny,
Why don't you eat people instead?'

Attendant in the Chamber of Horrors:
'Keep your husband moving, madam, we're stock-taking.'

Why did Henry VIII have so many wives?
He liked to chop and change.

RUDE JOKE RUDE JOKE RUDE JOKE RUDE JOKE RUDE JOKE RUDE JOKE RUDE
'My husband wants me to get him something
electrical for his birthday.'
'How about an electric chair?'
RUDE JOKE RUDE JOKE RUDE JOKE RUDE JOKE RUDE JOKE RUDE JOKE RUDE

A woman was walking along the beach with her
children, apparently searching for something.
   'Can I help you?' asked the lifeguard. 'You've
obviously lost something.'
   'Yes,' said the woman, 'it's my husband. The
children have buried him in the sand and I can't
find him.'
   'Can you remember where you were sitting?'
asked the lifeguard.
   'Don't be a fool,' said the woman. 'Can you
remember where you were sitting this time last year?'

How do you keep flies out of the kitchen?
Put a bucket of horse manure in the dining-room.

What do you call a man with no arms, legs or head,
floating up and down in the sea?
Bob.

228

'I don't think much of your wife.'
'Well, just eat the peas and potatoes.'

'Daddy, Daddy, I don't want to go to Australia.'
'Shut up and keep digging.'

What did the cannibal say when he saw the
missionary asleep?
'I just love breakfast in bed.'

'I got a pair of shoes for my husband.'
'Gosh, that was a good exchange.'

'Mummy, Mummy, I'm missing Daddy.'
'Shut up and reload your gun.'

TALL ORDERS

WANTED - Modern gas cooker suitable for bachelor with white enamel sides.

HELP WANTED: Man to handle explosives. Must be prepared to travel unexpectedly.

INTELLIGENT young lady required. Must speak proper and have good speling.

PIANO: Would suit a beginner with chipped legs.

UNEMPLOYED man seeks work. Completely honest and trustworthy, will take anything.

AMAZING OFFER: Fish and chip fryer, made from chip-resistant enamel.

LOST: An antique brooch depicting Venus in Shepherd's Bush on Saturday night.

FOR SALE: One collapsible baby in good condition.

DELIGHTFUL COUNTRY COTTAGE, two bedrooms, large lounge, kitchen, bathroom, coloured suite, toilet five miles from Tunbridge Wells.

FOR SALE: Delicate porcelain statuette. Victorian. Belongs to old lady slightly cracked.

A YOUNG LADY wants washing and cleaning three days a week.

ROOM WANTED for gentleman with good view and gas stove.

PLEASE NOTE: Rings can be ordered by post. Simply state size required or enclose string tied around your finger.

BICYCLE available for quick sale, looked after by young boy with three speeds and a collapsible frame.

FOR SALE: Beautiful lace wedding dress. Only worn twice.

FOR SALE: Genuine synthetic wigs. Real 100% man-made fibre, perfectly natural. Looks just like real hair. Colours red, green, mauve, orange, blue. No one will know it's not your own hair.

WASH AND SET, special offer: we will blow dry pensioners free on Wednesdays.

SECRETARY required. Shorthand essential but not absolutely necessary.

FOAM CUSHIONS - as an introduction to the rubber trade we offer foam rubber cushions at rock bottom prices.

VINTAGE WINES for sale, being the property of a lady moved from a cellar in Brighton.

FOR SALE: Baby boiler in perfect working order.

DONALD'S DAIRY - try our eggs. You can't beat them.

VISIT ALMA'S LAUNDRY - Leave your clothes with us while you go off shopping.

LADY with deaf aid wishes to meet gentleman with contact lenses.

ALLIGATOR FOR SALE. Would exchange for wooden leg.

FOR RENT: Two bedroom flatlet, fully furnished, bath two minutes' walk from railway station.

SAW MILL manager requires extra hands.

AUDITIONS for 'Snow White and the Seven Dwarfs'. Small parts only available.

ERRORS. No responsibility can be accepted for losses arising from typographical errors. Advertisers are expected to check their smalls to ensure correct appearance.

JUST JOKING

'Madam, your husband is lying unconscious in the hall beside a large package.'
'Oh good, my new hat has arrived!'

'We live on a houseboat.'
'Any special reason?'
'Yes, when we get short of money it's so easy to get to the bank.'

What is the best way to stop someone smoking?
Light their cigarette at both ends.

SCHOOLGIRL: Look, Miss, I've just painted your portrait. Don't you think it looks just like you?
ART TEACHER: Er … well … yes … it probably looks better from a distance.
SCHOOLGIRL: You see, I told you it looked just like you.

RUDE JOKE RUDE JOKE RUDE JOKE RUDE JOKE RUDE JOKE RUDE JOKE RUDE
Two birds were sitting in a tree when they saw Concorde fly over.
   'I wish I could fly as fast as that,' said one bird.
   'You would if your bottom was on fire,' said the other.

RUDE JOKE RUDE JOKE RUDE JOKE RUDE JOKE RUDE JOKE RUDE JOKE RUDE

233

TEACHER: I hope you understand the importance of the word 'punctuation'.
PUPIL: Oh, yes, sir. I always get to school on time.

MRS NEVILL: Today I broke a very expensive vase.
MRS FOX: Whatever did your husband say?
MRS NEVILL: 'Ouch! What hit me?'

'Money doesn't mean anything to me. My health is far more important.'
'Good. This is a stick-up. Your money or your life!'

What did the artist Whistler say when he found his mother wasn't in her rocking chair?
Hey, mother, you're off your rocker.'

DOCTOR FRANKENSTEIN: Where is the monster?
IGOR: He's gone to post seventeen Father's Day cards.

'Where is your brother?'
'In the house playing a piano duet. I finished first!'

Is it easy to milk a cow?
Yes, any little jerk can do it.

'I had bad sight until I was fifteen.'
'Then what happened?'
'I had my fringe cut.'

GRANDMA (*leaning over pram*): Oh you are such an adorable baby. I could eat you all up.
BABY: What, with no teeth?

What goes over a bridge with water above and
    water below, but doesn't get wet?
A woman with a bucket of water on her head.

What is sweet, has custard and is bad-tempered?
Apple grumble.

RUDE JOKE RUDE JOKE RUDE JOKE RUDE JOKE RUDE JOKE RUDE JOKE RUDE
At a children's picnic a little girl badly needed to go
to the toilet. She went behind a bush and, to her
distress, sat down on a thistle.
    Later that day she happened to see a little boy
going to the toilet, and she said to her mother:
    'Now that's a handy thing to take on a picnic.'
RUDE JOKE RUDE JOKE RUDE JOKE RUDE JOKE RUDE JOKE RUDE JOKE RUDE

What do you call a man sitting under a pile of leaves?
Russell.

What do you call a man who's been under a pile of
leaves for a hundred years?
Pete.

What did the bald man say when he received a
comb for Christmas?
'Thank you, I'll never part with it.'

'Have you a ladies' waiting-room on this station?'
'No, madam, but we have a room for ladies who can't wait.'

ED: My uncle is so rich that he owns a newspaper.
TED: So what? A newspaper only costs 20p.

'But why did you buy me such a small diamond?'
'I didn't want the glare to hurt your eyes.'

BILLY: I've just got myself a calendar.
TILLY: Why's that?
BILLY: Last week I pretended I was sick so that I wouldn't have to go to school; then I found out it was Saturday.

HEADMASTER: Now then Gladys, what were you doing behind the bicycle sheds after school yesterday? I want an explanation and the truth.
GLADYS: Do you want both of them?

'Can you lend me five pounds for a week, old dear?'
'Who's the weak old dear then?'

'But Angus, this isn't our baby!'
'Shut up, it's a better pram.'

236

OUT OF THIS WORLD

Down the street his funeral goes,
As sobs and wails diminish.
He died through drinking varnish,
But he had a lovely finish.

Epitaph From Australia
God took our flower
Our little Nell.
He thought he too
Would like a smell.

There was an old lady of Ryde
Who ate some green apples and died.
The apples fermented
Inside the lamented
And made cider inside her inside.

Mary Ann's Epitaph
Mary Ann has gone to rest
Safe at last on Abraham's breast,
Which may be nice for Mary Ann,
But it's certainly tough on Abraham.

Alice Mary Johnson 1883–1947
Let her RIP.

He passed the policeman without fuss,
And he passed the cart of hay,
He tried to pass a swerving bus,
And then he passed away.

Here lies ANN MANN;
She lived an old maid
And died an old Mann.
1819—1893

237

Erected to the memory of
JOHN MacFARLENE
Drowned in the waters of Leith
By a few affectionate friends.

Here lies the body of
MARY ANN LOWDER
Who died through drinking Seidlitz Powder.
She couldn't wait till it effervesced
So now she's gone to eternal rest.

Swans sing before they die;
'Twould be no bad thing,
If certain people had the grace
To die before they sing.

In crossing o'er the fatal bridge
John Morgan he was slain.
It was not by a mortal hand
But by a railway train.

RUDE JOKE RUDE JOKE RUDE JOKE RUDE JOKE RUDE JOKE RUDE JOKE RUDE
I had written to Aunt Maud,
Who was on a trip abroad,
When I heard she'd died of cramp -
Just too late to save the stamp.
RUDE JOKE RUDE JOKE RUDE JOKE RUDE JOKE RUDE JOKE RUDE JOKE RUDE

Epitaph Of A Fat Man
Here lies a man who met his fate
Because he put on too much weight.
To over-eating he was prone
But now he's gained his final STONE.

My wife is dead, and here she lies;
Nobody laughs, nobody cries.
Where she has gone, or how she fares,
Nobody knows, and nobody cares.

Joan Trueman
Here lies crafty Joan, deny it who can,
Who lived a false maid, and died a Trueman;
And this trick she had to make up her cunning,
Whilst one leg stood still, the other was running.

      Here lies a chump who got no gain
      From jumping off a moving train.
      Banana skins on platform seven
      Ensured his terminus was Heaven.

RUDE JOKE RUDE JOKE RUDE JOKE RUDE JOKE RUDE JOKE RUDE JOKE RUDE
I plant this shrub on your grave, dear wife,
So something on this spot has life.
Shrubs will wither, earth must rot;
Shrubs may revive: but you, thank heaven, will not!
RUDE JOKE RUDE JOKE RUDE JOKE RUDE JOKE RUDE JOKE RUDE JOKE RUDE

      Here lies the body of JOHN MOUND
      Who was lost at sea and never found.

Old Bill is gone too soon alas!
He tried to trace escaping gas.
With lighted match he braved the fates
Which blew him to the pearly gates.

      Epitaph of John Knott
      Here lies a man that was Knott born
      His father was Knott before him.
      He lived Knott, and did Knott die,
      Yet underneath this stone does lie;
      Knott christened,
      Knott begot,
      And here he lies,
      And yet was Knott.

Underneath this pile of stones
Lie the remains of Mary Jones.
Her name was Lloyd, it was not Jones,
But Jones was put to rhyme with stones.

Here lies the body of our MP
Who promised lots for you and me.
His words his deeds did not fulfil
And though he's dead he's LYING STILL.

Little Willie in the best of sashes
Played with fire and was burnt to ashes.
Very soon the room got chilly,
But no one liked to poke poor Willie.

STILL MORE KNOCK-KNOCKS

RUDE JOKE RUDE JOKE RUDE JOKE RUDE JOKE RUDE JOKE RUDE JOKE RUDE

Knock, knock.
Who's there?
Lucy.
Lucy who?
Lucy lastic. That's why they fell down!

RUDE JOKE RUDE JOKE RUDE JOKE RUDE JOKE RUDE JOKE RUDE JOKE RUDE

Knock, knock.
Who's there?
Europe.
Europe who?
Europe early this morning, can't you sleep?

Knock, knock.
Who's there?
Sir.
Sir who?
Sir View-Wright.

Knock, knock.
Who's there?
Butcher.
Butcher who?
Butcher left leg in, your left leg out ...

Knock, knock.
Who's there?
Olive.
Olive who?
Olive here, so let me in!

RUDE JOKE RUDE JOKE RUDE JOKE RUDE JOKE RUDE JOKE RUDE JOKE RUDE
Knock, knock.
Who's there?
Sonya.
Sonya who?
Sonya foot, I can smell it from here.
RUDE JOKE RUDE JOKE RUDE JOKE RUDE JOKE RUDE JOKE RUDE JOKE RUDE

Knock, knock.
Who's there?
Mayonnaise.
Mayonnaise who?
Mayonnaise have seen the glory of the coming of
the Lord.

Knock, knock.
Who's there?
Tish.
Tish who?
Tishoo, all fall down.

Knock, knock.
Who's there?
Walter.
Walter who?
Walter wall carpets are much more cosy.

Knock, knock.
Who's there?
Toothy.
Toothy who?
Toothy ith the day before Wednethday.

Knock, knock.
Who's there?
Nick.
Nick who?
Nick R. Elastic.

Knock, knock.
Who's there?
Constance Norah.
Constance Norah who?
Constance Norahs make it difficult to sleep.

Knock, knock.
Who's there?
Rabbit.
Rabbit who?
Rabbit up nicely, it's a present.

EXPELLED PUPILS

TEACHER: Why are you chewing gum in my
    lesson?
PUPIL: The shop had run out of toffees.

BOY: I didn't like that shepherd's pie.
DINNER LADY: I'll have you know I've been
    making shepherd's pies since before you were
    born.
BOY: Yeah, and I think that was one of them.

What do you call an art teacher who always
complains?
Mona Lisa.

GIRL: My sister and I know every word in the
    English dictionary.
TEACHER: What does somnambulism mean?
GIRL: That's one of the words my sister knows.

MOTHER: Sit down and tell me what your school
    report is like.
SON: I can't sit down. I just told Dad what my
    school report is like.

TEACHER: How do we know that carrots are good
   for eyesight?
PUPIL: Because you never see a rabbit wearing
   glasses.

Why is 1 + 1 = 3 like your left foot?
Because it's not right.

FATHER: What position do you play in football?
SON: Teacher says I'm the drawback.

What do you get if you cross a teacher with a monk
who has rolled in the mud?
A teacher with a dirty habit.

TEACHER: Neville, you always get everything
   wrong. I can't see how you're going to get a job
   when you leave school.
NEVILLE: Easily! I'm going to be a weather
   forecaster.

MRS A: What's your son going to be when he
   leaves school?
MRS B: About forty-five the rate he's going.

What happens to a pupil who misses the school bus
every day?
He catches it when he gets to school.

What's the difference between a pupil that talks a
lot in class and a book?
You can shut the book up.

MOTHER: I think Monica should have an
   encyclopaedia.
FATHER: Let her walk to school like everybody
   else.

MOTHER: How was your cookery lesson?
DAUGHTER: Awful. I was sent out of the class because I burnt something.
MOTHER: That wasn't very fair. What did you burn?
DAUGHTER: The classroom.

TEACHER: Find America on the map for me, Nigel.
NIGEL: It's here, Miss.
TEACHER: Good. Now, Timothy, tell me who discovered America?
TIMOTHY: Nigel did.

FATHER: Did you get the highest marks in your class today?
SON: No, Dad, do you get the highest salary in your office?

BRIAN: My parents are sending me to boarding school.
FELICITY: Why's that?
BRIAN: So that they won't have to help me with my homework.

PUPIL: Are slugs nice to eat, Miss?
TEACHER: Don't talk about such disgusting things at the dinner table. Get on with your meal and keep quiet.
(*After lunch*)
TEACHER: Now, what was all that nonsense about slugs?
PUPIL: Oh, it doesn't matter now, Miss. It's just that there was one in your salad, but it's gone now.

TEACHER: Where was the Declaration of Independence signed?
PUPIL: At the bottom, sir.

TEACHER: Did you write this poem all by
  yourself?
PUPIL: Yes, Miss.
TEACHER: Every single word of it?
PUPIL: Yes, Miss.
TEACHER: Then I'm delighted to meet you, Emily
  Brontë.

OUTRAGEOUS ANIMALS

What has a black cape, crawls through the night and bites people?
A tired mosquito wearing a black cape.

What do you get if you cross a hedgehog with a giraffe?
A ten-foot long toothbrush.

What do you get if you cross a squirrel with a kangaroo?
An animal that carries nuts in its pocket.

Why was the crab arrested?
It was always pinching things.

Did the geese get hurt when they crashed into each other?
No, they just had a few goose bumps.

What do you call a bald rabbit?
Hareless.

'I've just been out hunting. I caught five rabbits and a potfer.'
'What's a potfer?'
'To cook the rabbits in.'

What is black and white and noisy?
A zebra with a set of drums.

How do you stop a skunk from smelling?
Hold its nose.

What do you call ten angry dolphins?
Cross porpoises.

What did the beaver say to the tree?
It's been nice gnawing you.

What is white, furry and smells of peppermint?
A polo bear.

How did the chimpanzee escape from its cage?
With a monkey wrench.

Why is a cat longer at night than in the morning?
Because he's let out at night and taken in again in the morning.

If a quadruped has four legs and a biped has two legs, what is a zebra?
A stri-ped.

BOY: Do you sell dog's bones?
BUTCHER: Only if they're with an adult.

What do you get if you cross a cow with a camel?
Lumpy milkshakes.

Which animal talks a lot?
A yak.

Which animal talks the most?
A yakety-yak.

Did you hear about the lion with pedestrian eyes?
They look both ways before they cross.

Which animals use nut-crackers?
Toothless squirrels.

Why did the cock refuse to fight?
Because he was chicken.

What do you get if you cross a crab with a maths teacher?
Snappy answers.

What do sheep wear when they go to school?
Ewe-niforms.

Why shouldn't you cry when a cow trips over?
It's no good crying over spilt milk.

CUSTOMER: Have you any wild duck?
WAITER: No, but we have a tame one we can
   irrritate for you.

'Have you put the cat out?'
'Yes, I just trod on its tail.'

What do you call a bee born in May?
A maybe.

What did the buffalo say to his son when he went
off on a long journey?
'Bison!'

RUDE JOKE RUDE JOKE RUDE JOKE RUDE JOKE RUDE JOKE RUDE JOKE RUDE
What has four legs and flies?
A dead elephant.
RUDE JOKE RUDE JOKE RUDE JOKE RUDE JOKE RUDE JOKE RUDE JOKE RUDE

'ORRIBLE ODES

Mary had a little car,
She drove in manner deft.
But every time she signalled right,
The little car turned left.

The rain it raineth on the just,
And also on the unjust fella;
But chiefly on the just, because,
The unjust steals the just's umbrella!

'Twixt the optimist and the pessimist
The difference is quite droll.
The optimist sees the doughnut
While the pessimist sees the hole.

Ooey Gooey was a worm,
A wondrous worm was he.
He stepped upon the railway track,
A train he did not see.
Ooey Gooey.

Some say that fleas are black,
But I know that is not so,
'Cos Mary had a little lamb
With fleas as white as snow.

A handsome young airman lay dying,
And as on the airfield he lay,
To the mechanics who round him came
    sighing,
These last dying words did he say:
'Take the cylinders out of my kidneys,
The connecting rod out of my brain,
Take the camshaft out of my backbone,
And assemble the engine again.'

The night was growing old
As she trudged through snow and sleet;
And her nose was long and cold,
And her shoes were full of feet.

Here I sit in the moonlight,
Abandoned by women and men,
Muttering over and over,
'I'll never eat garlic again.'

When I die, bury me deep,
Bury my history book at my feet.
Tell the teacher I've gone to rest,
And won't be back for the history test.

New Proverb:
Early to bed
And early to rise
Makes you feel stupid
And gives you red eyes.

Eaper Weaper, chimney-sweeper,
Had a wife but couldn't keep her,
Had anovver, didn't love her,
So up the chimney he did shove her.

Newton heard a sort of plonk -
An apple fell upon his conk;
Discovering gravitation law
Shook old Isaac to the core.

> Little Miss Muffet
> Sat on her tuffet
> Eating her Irish stew.
> Along came a spider
> And sat down beside her,
> So she ate him up too.

RUDE JOKE RUDE JOKE RUDE JOKE RUDE JOKE RUDE JOKE RUDE JOKE RUDE
Lillie paid two-fifty for
A little floral pinafore;
Surprising what a lot it hides
Since she wears nothing else besides!
RUDE JOKE RUDE JOKE RUDE JOKE RUDE JOKE RUDE JOKE RUDE JOKE RUDE

> Sweet little Eileen Rose
> Was tired and sought some sweet repose.
> But her sister Clare
> Put a pin upon her chair
> And sweet little Eileen rose.

Mary had a little bear
To which she was so kind,
And everywhere that Mary went
You saw her bear running along beside her!

> I wish I was a little grub
> With whiskers round my tummy
> I'd climb into a honey pot
> And make my tummy gummy.

KITCHEN CHAOS

If a woman is slicing meat and some falls on the floor, what would you call it?
A slip of the tongue.

'There's no steak in this steak pie!'
'Well you don't get cottage in cottage pie or dog in dog meat, so what are you complaining about?'

CUSTOMER: Why is it that I never get what I ask for here?
WAITER: Perhaps, madam, because we are too polite.

'This restaurant is historic. Almost everything here has its legend.'
'Let's ask about this steak; I'm sure it's got a long history.'

DINER (*beckoning to waiter*): Excuse me, waiter, is it raining outside?
WAITER: Sorry, sir, this is not my table.

'Waiter, waiter, why have you got your thumb on my steak?'
'I don't want to drop it on the floor again.'

'Waiter, waiter, there's a dead beetle in my wine.'
'You asked for something with a little body in it, sir.'

'Waiter, waiter, what is this soup?'
'It's bean soup, sir'.
'I don't care what it's been. What is it now?'

'Why did that man get angry while you were eating the ploughman's lunch?'
'Perhaps he was the ploughman.'

What is the best way to stop rice sticking together?
Boil each grain separately.

What is the best way to serve leftovers?
Serve them to somebody else.

FRED: How is your onion diet going? Have you lost anything?
MILDRED: Half a stone and half a dozen friends.

'Waiter, waiter, how long have you worked here?'
'Two weeks, sir.'
'Then it can't be you that took my order.'

'Waiter, waiter, bring me a chicken and make sure it is as young as possible.'
'How about a new-laid egg, sir?'

WAITER: And what will you have after your main course, madam?
CUSTOMER: If it's like the last meal I had here, it will be indigestion.

'Waiter, waiter, there's a bee in my soup.'
'It's alphabet soup, sir.'

HEAD TEACHER: Johnny, why are you the only
   boy in the class today?
JOHNNY: I was the only one that didn't have
   school dinner yesterday.

What sort of meat do idiots like?
Chump chops.

If a chicken drank whisky, what would it lay?
Scotch eggs.

'Waiter, waiter, do you serve a balanced diet?'
'Nothing's ever fallen off the plate yet, sir.'

'Waiter, waiter, is the food here good?'
'I'm a waiter, sir, not a witness.'

MOTHER: Wash those fish well before you cook them.
SCOUT: Why wash something that's spent its
   whole life in water?

CUSTOMER: What does one have to do to get a
   glass of water here?
WAITER: Set fire to yourself.

What is the fish frier's favourite motto?
If at first you don't succeed, fry, fry and fry again.

INSULTS

ALBERT: You've got a face like a million dollars.
CYNTHIA: Why, thank you.
ALBERT: Yes, all green and wrinkled.

BOY: Sir, I would like to marry your daughter.
FATHER: Why tell me your troubles?

'Did the new play have a happy ending?'
'Yes, everybody was happy when it finished.'

'I'm nobody's fool.'
'Well, maybe you can get someone to adopt you.'

NAUGHTY NIGEL: My sister has musical feet.
CRAZY CHRISTINE: How's that?
NAUGHTY NIGEL: They're both flat.

CECIL: Why do you call your boyfriend laryngitis?
KAREN: Because he's a pain in the neck.

The rain makes all things beautiful,
The grass and flowers too.
If rain makes all things beautiful
Why don't it rain on you?

BILL: Did your singing teacher really say that your voice was heavenly?

NELL: Almost. He said it was like nothing on earth.

HARVEY: If you don't say you'll marry me I'll hang myself from that tree in front of your house.

VERONICA: You know my father doesn't like you hanging around.

CELIA: Is your boyfriend clever?

GLADYS: Clever? He couldn't tell which direction a lift was going even if he had two guesses.

'Who's that little lady with the wart?'
'She's his wife!'

HORACE: I've seen you somewhere before.

ACTRESS: Probably in the theatre?

HORACE: Oh, yes, you sell the pop-corn, don't you?

'Can you lend me 10p; I want to telephone a friend.'
'Here's 20p. Ring both of them.'

FATHER: I never told lies when I was a boy.

SON: At what age did you begin?

'Is that your real face, or are you still wearing a gas mask?'

When their first child was born a man turned to his wife and said:

'Good, now we can call your mother Grandma, instead of "Oi! You!"'

'Whenever we have a collection he's the first to put his hand in … a sling!'

JULIA: I wish I had a penny for every boy that has asked me out.

JULIAN: At least you'd be able to go to the toilet, if nothing else.

MILDRED: I'll have you know that I've got the face of an eighteen-year-old.

MICHAEL: Well give it back, you're getting it all wrinkled.

'How nice to see you. You haven't changed in years.'
'No, the laundry's been on strike.'

'What was the funniest thing you ever saw?'
'The first time you walked into a room.'

FRANK: This hat fits really well.

ALICE: Yes, but what will you do when your ears get tired?

'I'd like to see something cheap in hats.'
'Put some on and look in the mirror!'

VICAR: Now stop fighting you two. You should
    love your enemy.
BOY: He's not my enemy; he's my brother.

'Everything I say to you goes in one ear and out the
other.'
'That's why God gave us two ears.'

'I've got a bad stomach.'
'Well, keep your coat buttoned and maybe nobody
will notice.'

NAUGHTY STORIES

NAUGHTY NIGEL: What does your dad do for a living?
BAD BERYL: He collects fleas.
NAUGHTY NIGEL: What does your mother do?
BAD BERYL: Scratch.

'How do you spell rain?'
'R-A-N-E.'
'That's the worst spell of rain we've had around here for a long time.'

MICHAEL: Do you know anyone that's been on the telly?
WILLIAM: Only my dog, but that was before he was housetrained.

HEADMISTRESS: This is the fourth time this week you've been brought to me to be punished. What have you got to say for yourself?
SCHOOLBOY: Thank goodness it's Friday.

MOTHER: Why have you got cotton wool in one ear? Have you got earache?
SON: No, Teacher says everything she says goes in one ear and out the other, so I'm trying to stop it.

BOARDING SCHOOL MASTER: Are you
    homesick?
SCHOOLBOY: No, I'm here sick.

'Say, who do you think you're pushing?'
'I don't know. What's your name?'

ALICE: My little brother just fell down a manhole;
    what shall I do?
PASSER-BY: Run into the library and get a book on
    how to raise a child.

'Is your brother well-behaved?'
'Oh yes, he always takes his shoes off before
putting his feet on the table.'

Why are maggots like naughty children?
Because they wriggle out of things.

Why did the boy take an axe to school?
It was breaking up day.

NAUGHTY NICHOLAS: My sister has a
    photographic memory.
MISCHIEVOUS MICHAEL: That must be very
    useful.
NAUGHTY NICHOLAS: Not really, nothing ever
    seems to develop.

Poor old teacher. We missed you so
When into hospital you did go.
For you to remain would be a sin;
We're sorry about the banana skin.

BOY: Dad, can I have another glass of water?
FATHER: But that's the eighth glass in five minutes.
BOY: I know, but my bedroom's on fire.

FATHER: Timmy, what happened to that
unbreakable, waterproof, rustproof, shockproof,
anti-magnetic, everlasting watch I gave you for
your birthday?
TIMMY: I lost it.

Why did the naughty boy put wheels on his
grandfather's rocking chair?
He wanted to see him rock 'n' roll.

What did the thief say to the watchmaker?
Sorry to have taken so much of your valuable time.

What animal can you never trust?
A cheetah.

'Will you be using your lawn mower this
afternoon?'
'Yes.'
'All afternoon?'
'Yes.'
'Good, I can borrow your tennis racket then.'

Why is it rude to whisper?
Because it is not aloud.

MOTHER: Did you make someone happy today?
WILY WILLIE: Yes, Mum. I went to see Aunt
  Gladys, and when I left she was happy.

NELLY: Where do you take your baths?
NIKKI: In the spring.
NELLY: I said 'where' not 'when'.

Naughty Piece of Advice:
Keep smiling, it makes everybody wonder what
you've been up to!

TEACHER: Now Boswell, you shouldn't fight. You
  must learn to give and take.
BOSWELL: I did give and take. I gave him a black
  eye and took his bag of toffees.

TERRIBLE TONGUE-TWISTERS

What is a tongue-twister?
It's when your tang gets all tongulled up.

The prattling prig pranced around the prairie and
played his ukulele to the priest.

If a Hottentot taught
A Hottentot tot,
To talk ere the tot could totter,
Ought the Hottentot tot
Be taught to say 'ought' or 'nought'
Or what ought to be taught to her?

Mrs Cripp's cat crept into the crypt, crept around
and out through the crack.

A selfish shellfish smelt a stale fish.
If the stale fish was a smelt
Then the selfish shellfish smelt a smelt.

Whistle for the thistle sifter.

Stop Chop shops selling Chop Shop chops.

Betty Batter had some butter,
'But,' she said, 'this butter's bitter.
If I bake this bitter butter,
It would make my batter bitter.'

Two Shetland shepherds share the Shetland
shawl.

My Miss Smith lisps and lists.
She lisps as she talks and she lists as she walks.

'Aye! Aye!' said the ear.
'Here! Here!' said the eye.

Say this sharply, say this sweetly,
Say this shortly, say this softly,
Say this sixteen times in succession.

Ninety-nine naughty knitted nick-nacks were
nicked by ninety-nine naughty knitted nick-nack
nickers!

Please, Paul, pause for applause.

If a woodchuck could chuck wood,
How much wood would a woodchuck chuck,
If a woodchuck could chuck wood?

Ned Nott was shot
And Sam Shott was not.
So it is better to be Shott
    than Nott.
Some say Nott
    was not shot.
But Shott says
    he shot Nott.
Either the shot Shott shot at Nott
    was not shot,
    or
    Nott was shot.
If the shot Shott shot shot Shott,
    then Shott was shot,
    not Nott.
However,
    the shot Shott shot shot not Shott -
    but Nott.

I snuff shop snuff.
Do you shop at the snuff shop for shop snuff?
I snuff enough snuff to stock a snuff shop!

His shirt soon shrank in the suds.

Can you imagine,
an imaginary menagerie manager
imagining managing an imaginary
menagerie?

Elizabeth lisps lengthy lessons.

I thought a thought.
But the thought I thought wasn't
    the thought I thought I thought.
If the thought I thought I thought
    had been the thought I thought,
I wouldn't have thought so much.

A maid with a duster made a furious bluster
Dusting a bust in the hall.
When the bust it was dusted the bust it was busted,
The bust it was dust, that's all!

HOSPITAL HORRORS

'Doctor, Doctor, will you give me something for my head?'
'Thanks, but I've already got one.'

ALBERT: My sister is going to be a nurse.
WINNIE: Her a nurse! She can't even put a
  dressing on a salad!

NURSE: Take this, it will give you nourishment.
PATIENT: I'm fed up with nourishment, nurse.
  Bring me some food!

'Doctor Killmore, this is the third operating table
you've ruined this month. You really must not cut
so deeply!'

DOCTOR: Did you drink the medicine after a hot
  bath?
PATIENT: No, I haven't finished the bath yet.

RECEPTIONIST: Dr Wanganoosipapodoopolis will
  see you now.
PATIENT: Which doctor?
RECEPTIONIST: Oh no, he's fully qualified.

RUDE JOKE RUDE JOKE RUDE JOKE RUDE JOKE RUDE JOKE RUDE JOKE RUDE
DOCTOR: Oh, you're American. In which state
  were you born?
PATIENT: In the nude.
RUDE JOKE RUDE JOKE RUDE JOKE RUDE JOKE RUDE JOKE RUDE JOKE RUDE

'Doctor, Doctor, I've got an upset stomach.'
'How many more times have I got to tell you not to
eat school dinners?'

'Doctor, Doctor, I need something for my kidney.'
'Here's a pound of steak;
make yourself a pie.'

DOCTOR: And what seems to be the trouble?
PATIENT: I keep thinking that when I speak
nobody can hear me.
DOCTOR: And what seems to be the trouble?

'Doctor, Doctor, I keep thinking that people are
ignoring me.'
'Next patient, please!'

'Doctor, Doctor, I think my eyesight is getting worse.'
'I think it is; this is the Post Office.'

What is the definition of a doctor?
A man who suffers from good health.

DOCTOR: I'm terry sorry Mrs Hargreaves, but I'm
afraid you have rabies.
PATIENT: Quick, give me a pen and paper.
DOCTOR: Why, do you wish to make a will?
PATIENT: No, a list of people that I want to bite.

'Doctor, Doctor, what is the best thing to take when
you feel run down?'
'The number of the car.'

What kind of doctor has a nasty temper?
One with no patients.

DOCTOR: How are the pills that I gave you to
improve your memory?
PATIENT: What pills?

Did you hear about the boy who wanted to be a
doctor but his handwriting was too neat?

DOCTOR: How did you break your neck?
PATIENT: I followed your prescription just as you
told me.
DOCTOR: How did that break your neck?
PATIENT: It blew out of the back of the bus.

'Doctor, Doctor, how can I stop losing my hair?'
'Sew a name tag inside your wig.'

Did you hear about the cross-eyed doctor who
never saw eye-to-eye with his patients?

'Doctor, Doctor, I keep thinking I'm a fly.'
'Well come down from the ceiling and let's talk
about it.'

'Doctor, Doctor, I keep thinking that there are two of me.'
'One patient at a time, please.'

PATIENT: So the X-ray showed that I was perfectly normal?
DOCTOR: Oh yes, both your heads are fine.

DOCTOR: Have you been taking the pills three times a day?
VICAR: Yes, I followed your directions religiously.

RUDE JOKE RUDE JOKE RUDE JOKE RUDE JOKE RUDE JOKE RUDE JOKE RUDE
'Doctor, do you approve of eating everything raw?'
'No, always wear clothes, just in case you spill anything.'
RUDE JOKE RUDE JOKE RUDE JOKE RUDE JOKE RUDE JOKE RUDE JOKE RUDE

WALLS OF THE WILD

A STITCH IN TIME SAVES AN EMBARRASSING EXPOSURE!

I'VE GOT 'O' LEVELS IN HISTORY AND WOODWORK.
You can start making antique furniture!

THERE'S FAR TOO MUCH APATHY IN THIS COUNTRY.
Who cares?

I WAS GOING TO KILL MYSELF BY TAKING A BOTTLE OF
ASPIRINS - BUT AFTER THE FIRST TWO I FELT MUCH
BETTER.

YOU TOO CAN HAVE A BODY LIKE MINE.
Just lie down under a tractor.

IF ALL THE WORLD'S A STAGE AND MEN AND WOMEN ARE
MERELY PLAYERS, WHERE DOES THE AUDIENCE COME FROM?

HELP AUSTRALIAN OAKS.
Plant an acorn upside-down!

FOUND: ONE PAIR OF GLASSES
Please write larger, I've lost my glasses.

HAVE A STIFF DRINK; PUT CEMENT IN YOUR LEMONADE!

BAD LUCK IS BENDING OVER TO PICK UP A FOUR-LEAF
CLOVER AND GETTING INFECTED WITH POISON IVY!

I'M GOING TO TAKE UP MEDITATION.
Better than sitting around all day doing nothing.

BEETHOVEN WAS SO DEAF HE THOUGHT HE WAS A
PAINTER.

I HATE GRAFFITI!
I hate all Italian food.

THE WORLD WILL END ON FRIDAY.
I hadn't any plans for the weekend anyway.

THERE'S A HORROR AT THE CINEMA - I daren't buy an
ice-cream from her during the interval!

ISAAC NEWTON WAS RIGHT - THIS IS THE CENTRE OF
GRAFFITI.

NOTHING IS IMPOSSIBLE.
I've been doing nothing for years.

I HAVE TROUBLE CATCHING GROUSE.
You're not throwing your dog up high enough!

VISIT THE IRISH POST OFFICE TOWER.
The restaurant stays still and the diners walk round
in circles!

WE'RE GOING TO HAVE A NEW TV SET - THE PROGRAMMES
ON THE OLD ONE ARE DREADFUL.

HOW DOES A ONE-MAN BUS MOVE WHEN THE DRIVER IS
UPSTAIRS COLLECTING THE FARES?

BECOME A FLY AND STICK YOUR NOSE INTO OTHER
PEOPLE'S BUSINESS.

SELL PERFUME AND STICK YOUR BUSINESS INTO OTHER
PEOPLE'S NOSES.

CINDERELLA MARRIED FOR THE MONEY!
Bo Peep did it for the insurance!

EARN CASH IN YOUR SPARE TIME -
Blackmail your friends!

YESTERDAY I COULDN'T SPELL EDUCATED, NOW I ARE IT!

MY MOTHER HAD A NERVOUS BREAKDOWN TRYING TO FIT
ROUND TOMATOES INTO SQUARE SANDWICHES.

BE ALERT - YOUR COUNTRY NEEDS LERTS.
No, be aloof, we've got enough lerts.

THEY SAY AN ELEPHANT NEVER FORGETS, BUT WHAT'S AN
ELEPHANT GOT TO REMEMBER?

WHAT CAN I TAKE FOR KLEPTOMANIA?
Did you hear about the kleptomaniac's daughter?
She took after her mother.

I'VE BEEN CURED OF INDECISION - AT LEAST I THINK I
HAVE.

LIMERICK LAUGHS

When a sailor in Regent's Park zoo
Grabbed a seven-day-old kangaroo,
Its poor mother said, 'Jack,
You can put it right back.
You know picking my pocket's taboo.'

There was a young lady whose eyes
Were unique as to colour and size;
When she opened them wide,
People all turned aside,
And started away in surprise.

`

A girl who weighed many an ounce
Used language I dare not pronounce
For a fellow unkind
Pulled her chair out behind,
Just to see, so he said, if she'd bounce.

There was an old woman from China
Who once went to sea on a liner.
She fell off the deck
And twisted her neck
And now she can see right behind her.

There was once a man from Darjeeling
Who boarded a bus bound for Ealing.
It said on the door,
'Please don't spit on the floor',
So he stood up and spat on the ceiling.

There was an old lady whose folly
Induced her to sit on some holly,
Whereon by a thorn,
Her dress being torn,
She quickly became melancholy.

There was an old person of Dover,
Who rushed through a field of blue clover;
But some very large bees
Stung his nose and his knees,
So he very soon went back to Dover.

A daring young lady of Guam
Observed, 'The Pacific's so calm
I'll swim out for a lark.'
She met a large shark ...
Let us now sing the Ninetieth Psalm.

A jovial fellow named Packer
Pulled a joke out one day from a cracker.
It said, 'If you're stuck
For a turkey, try duck -
You could say it's a real Christmas quacker!'

A sleeper from the Amazon
Put nighties of his grandma's on.
The reason? That
He was too fat
To get his own pyjamazon.

I sat next to the duchess at tea,
It was just as I feared it would be.
Her rumblings abdominal
Were simply phenomenal
And everyone thought it was me!

There was a young lady of Oakham,
Who would steal cigarettes and then soak 'em
In honey and rum,
And then smear 'em with gum,
So it wasn't a pleasure to smoke 'em.

There was a young curate of Sarum,
Whose manners were quite harem-scarem:
He ran about Hants
Without any pants
Till his bishop compelled him to wear 'em.

A fellow named Malcolm MacHairs
Kept a number of grizzly bears.
He ran out of money
For they ate so much honey,
And then they ate Malcolm - who cares?

There was a young man of Bengal
Who went to a fancy dress ball.
He decided to risk it
And went as a biscuit,
But a dog ate him up in the hall.

There was an old maiden from Fife,
Who had never been kissed in her life;
Along came a cat,
So she said, 'I'll kiss that!'
But the cat answered, 'Not on your life!'

There was a young lady from Aenus
Who went to a party as Venus.
We told her how rude
'Twas to go there quite nude,
So we got her a leaf from the green-h'us.

Other titles available from Madcap:

Oink! The Pig Joke Book (scratch 'n' sniff)

Author: Sandy Ransford
Illustrator: Andy Hammond

Have you ever seen a pig fly? Well, keep your
snouts in the air, and your trotters on the ground.
These hilarious pig jokes will have you leaping
with laughter and squealing for more!

'I've just bought a pig.'
'But where will you keep it?'
'In the dining room.'
'But what about the smell and the mess?'
'Oh, the pig won't mind that.'

What do you put on a pig that comes out in a rash?
Oinkment!

Why did the piglets take no notice of their father?
Because he was an old boar!

The perfect joke book for pig fans everywhere,
trough-full of side-splitting gags, it will leave you
as happy as a pig in muck and chuckling so hard
you'll have to sow your sides up!

ISBN 0 233 99570 6

PRICE £3.50

The Rotten Eggs Joke Book (scratch 'n' sniff)

Author: Sandy Ransford
Illustrator: David Farris

This book stinks! It really does! Scratch the cover and you'll find out that it's not called *The Rotten Eggs Joke Book* for nothing.

And it's even whiffier inside – crammed with revolting jokes about rotten eggs and other smelly food, stinking socks, pongy animals, disgusting habits, reeking drains and, if that weren't enough, ghosts, ghouls and vampires to send shivers down your spine.

If you suffer from a nervous disposition or a queasy stomach, you may do better to leave it unopened. On the other hand, if you're brave enough and tough enough, you'll have the laugh of a lifetime!

ISBN 0 233 99088 7

PRICE £2.99

The Football Joke Book

Author: Clive Dickinson
Illustrator: David Farris

From the stadiums of the Premier League, to the waterlogged field behind the old gas works, you'll find jokes for the whole world of football – on the terraces, in the dressing room and on the journey back home.

What is common to both Alan Shearer and a magician?
A hat trick!

A little boy kept turning up at school wearing an Arsenal top. Finally the head teacher said to his mother, 'We don't mind him coming to school in a football top, but do you think you could get him to wear some shorts as well?'

What did the footballer say when he accidentally burped during a game?
Sorry, it was a freak hic!

It's all here – the action, the thrills, the goals, the highs, the lows and everything else you've ever wanted from the game. Get ready, then. The teams are in position. The ref's checking his watch and it's kick off!

ISBN 0 233 99377 0

PRICE £3.50

Madcap Pounders

Author: Gyles Brandreth

This weird and wonderful humour book series is great value at only a pound a book. There's plenty of choice, with something for everyone and many a chuckle along the way!

Titles available in the Madcap Pounders Series:

Crazy Crosswords	0 233 99320 7
Crazy Graffiti	0 233 99318 5
Crazy Hoaxes	0 233 99316 9
Crazy Howlers	0 233 99315 0
Crazy Inventions	0 233 99098 4
Crazy Jokes	0 233 99067 4
Crazy Practical Jokes	0 233 99095 X
Crazy Riddles	0 233 99319 3
Crazy Spy File	0 233 99063 1
Crazy Tongue Twisters	0 233 99317 7
Crazy Words	0 233 99097 6
Crazy World Records	0 233 99096 8

PRICE £1.00 each

The Knock Out! Knock Knock Joke Book

Author: Gyles Brandreth
Illustrator: John MacGregor

Introducing the biggest, the best, and the boldest knock-knock bonanza in the world, ever.

If you thought you'd heard them all, try these for size!

Knock, Knock.
Who's there?
Michelle.
Michelle who?
Michelle had a big crab inside it!

Knock, Knock.
Who's there?
Nose.
Nose who?
I Nose plenty more Knock-Knock Jokes!

For tongue-twistingly, side-splittingly good jokes which will knock you sideways, look no further than *The Knockout Knock-Knock Joke Book!*

ISBN 0 233 99376 2

PRICE £2.99

The Teddy Bear Joke Book

Author: Gyles Brandreth
Illustrator: Alan Snow

At last! A bear-shaped book full of unbearably funny jokes!

What's a polar bear's favourite breakfast?
Ice Crispies!

What do you call a teddy bear wearing five balaclavas?
Anything you want, he won't hear you!

Why was the teddy bear wearing dark glasses?
If you had so many jokes made about you, you wouldn't want to be recognised either!

Just how many can you bear?

ISBN 0 233 99089 5

PRICE £2.99

A Trunk Full of Laughs

Specially compiled by that award-winning writer
Ellie Phant, *A Trunk Full of Laughs* is a hilarious,
uproarious, side-splitting collection of jokes,
featuring crazy, zany animals from apes to zebras!

A herd of cows had formed an orchestra. What
were they called?
Moosicians!

What do you call a herd of elephants in a water-
hole?
Swimming trunks!

Why wouldn't the cockerel cross the busy road?
Because he was chicken!

ISBN 0 233 99062 3

PRICE £2.99

The Madcap Giant Book of Jokes

Author: Gyles Brandreth
Illustrator: David Farris

A huge, enormous, gigantic, vast collection of jokes,
puzzles and teasers; pranks and challenges for
hours and hours of amusement.

Doctor, Doctor, I need something for my liver.
Take this pound of onions!

Knock, knock.
Who's there?
N.E.
N.E.who?
N.E.body you like, as long as you let me in!

The biggest book of laughter you'll ever come
across.

ISBN 0 233 99192 1

PRICE £2.99

All these books are available at your local
bookshop. Alternatively, they can be ordered direct
from Harper Collins Publishers, Customer Services
Centre, PO Box, Glasgow, G4 0NB. Tel: 0141 306
3100, fax: 0141 306 3767.